# TRAPPED

# TRAPPED

## CAUGHT IN A LIE

## Melody Carlson

**NAVPRESS**

Discipleship Inside Out™

**Discipleship Inside Out™**

NavPress is the publishing ministry of The Navigators, an international Christian organization and leader in personal spiritual development. NavPress is committed to helping people grow spiritually and enjoy lives of meaning and hope through personal and group resources that are biblically rooted, culturally relevant, and highly practical.

**For a free catalog go to www.NavPress.com
or call 1.800.366.7788 in the United States or 1.800.839.4769 in Canada.**

NavPress titles may be purchased in bulk for ministry, educational, business, fund-raising, or sales promotional use. For information, please call NavPress Special Markets at 1.800.504.2924.

ISBN-13: 978-1-60006-951-2

Cover design by Faceout Studio, Charles Brock
Cover image by iStock

Published in association with the literary agency of Sara A. Fortenberry.

Some of the anecdotal illustrations in this book are true to life and are included with the permission of the persons involved. All other illustrations are composites of real situations, and any resemblance to people living or dead is coincidental.
Carlson, Melody.

  Trapped : caught in a lie / Melody Carlson.
      p. cm. -- (Secrets)
  Summary: "As straight-A student GraceAnn enters her senior year, the stakes seem higher, the stress is mounting, and after bad breakup with her boyfriend, her grades begin to slip. Couldn't she cheat, this just one time?"-- Provided by publisher.
  ISBN 978-1-60006-951-2 (pbk.)
  [1. Stress (Psychology)--Fiction. 2. Cheating--Fiction. 3. Christian life--Fiction. 4. High schools--Fiction. 5. Schools--Fiction. 6. Best friends--Fiction. 7. Friendship--Fiction.] I. Title.
  PZ7.C216637Tr 2012
  [Fic]--dc23
                                        2011046538

Printed in the United States of America

1 2 3 4 5 6 7 8 / 16 15 14 13 12

## OTHER NOVELS BY MELODY CARLSON

SECRETS Series

*Damaged*

*Forgotten*

*Shattered*

TRUECOLORS Series

*Bitter Rose*

*Blade Silver*

*Bright Purple*

*Burnt Orange*

*Dark Blue*

*Deep Green*

*Faded Denim*

*Fool's Gold*

*Harsh Pink*

*Moon White*

*Pitch Black*

*Torch Red*

If anyone asks my opinion on categorizing personality types, I claim to be totally against labeling people and will say that everyone should be respected as an individual and not pigeon-holed. But the truth is, I know I have a type A personality. In fact, I sometimes take the free online personality tests, and unless I cheat on my answers, which would be wrong, I score frighteningly high.

In all honesty, I am an uncompromising perfectionist who flirts with a tendency toward OCD (obsessive-compulsive disorder). But will I admit this to anyone? Of course not. Because underneath my obsession with perfection is a very insecure little girl. A little girl who knows she does not measure up . . . and probably never will.

An ironic side of my type A obsessions is how much effort I put into my psychotic attempts to disguise myself as easygoing and laid back, like a type B. Crazy as it sounds, sometimes I almost manage to convince myself that I really am this carefree and unmotivated person. Or maybe I just hope acting like that will change me somehow. But my underlying feeling is that it's hopeless. I was wired to be intense and competitive and bossy. That's just the way my DNA dice were tossed. Unfortunately, this can be hard on relationships . . . and boyfriends.

"You're too high maintenance," Clayton told me just last week.

"High maintenance? What are you talking about?"

"You're difficult, GraceAnn. You make everything harder than it needs to be. And it just gets old after a while. You know?" He peered at me with those big brown eyes, those sweet puppy-dog eyes, and I was ready to agree with him—and to be fair, he was probably right. But for some reason I just couldn't back down. I mean, what girl wants her boyfriend to call her "difficult"?

Besides, Clayton had promised to pick me up by seven o'clock. I'd rushed home from work, taken a shower, done my hair, and put myself back together—all in less than an hour. And at a few minutes before seven, I was ready to go. But Clayton didn't pull up until 7:28, which in my opinion is too late to make the 7:40 movie. And maybe that's my problem, because I hate to be late. But my idea of a good movie date is having my popcorn and soda in hand and being seated in a good spot in the theater just as the lights go down. Is that too much to ask? According to Clayton, it is.

"You think *I'm* difficult?" I tried to keep my voice calm and easygoing despite my rising blood pressure. "What about you? You're late and—"

"I was a few minutes late—because of traffic—and you throw a complete hissy fit," he snapped back at me.

"A few minutes?" I held out my watch to make a point. "Maybe you haven't learned how to tell time yet." Okay, that might've been a bit harsh.

And so, on we went, arguing like an old married couple until Clayton literally threw his hands in the air and proclaimed that we needed to take a break.

"What do you mean by a break? Like break up?"

"I don't know, GraceAnn." He shrugged and looked down at his shoes like he was thinking it over. "I need a little break from your constant whining."

Well, that just totally ticked me off. I mean, he was the one nearly half an hour late, yet he was accusing me of whining and being difficult.

"Fine," I told him. "Let's take a break — in fact, while we're at it, let's just break up, Clayton. Let's throw in the towel, call it quits, *finito*." Okay, I thought that would get his attention. Because I honestly believed Clayton loved me as much as I loved him, and I thought he would apologize and beg me to reconsider.

"Maybe that's a good idea," he said way too easily. "For both of us." Then he leaned over and pecked me on the cheek, headed back to his truck, and just drove away. End of story.

Well, not quite . . . because now I'm pining away for him. Secretly, of course, because I don't want anyone to know how deeply I'm hurt. Well, except for Rory, my faithful canine companion. I tell him everything. Rory is part golden retriever. And for seven years he's slept in my bed almost every night. I've had him since I was ten, and I seriously don't know what I'd do without my Rory.

Well, Rory and my best friend, Mary Beth. Mary Beth and I have been best friends for ages . . . probably starting back in grade school when we both got teased for having double names. Geoff Landers said we were "rednecks" and sometimes called us both Daisy May just to be mean. But that only tightened our allegiance to each other.

I don't know what I'd do without Mary Beth. And yet I still haven't admitted to her just how heartbroken I am over Clayton.

Instead I've kept up a brave front, pretending the breakup was mutual. And really, wasn't it? As I recall, I was the one who brought up the idea in the first place. So seriously, why should I be upset? Yeah, right.

"You're taking it so well," Mary Beth told me after youth group on Sunday night. It was just one day after the breakup, and I was acting like it was no big deal. "I'm really impressed, GraceAnn. I thought you'd be a basket case by now."

"God is helping me with it," I told her. And I wanted to believe that was true. Unfortunately, it might've been my spiritual pride talking, trying to appear stronger than I was, maybe even for the rest of youth group to see. It hadn't helped that Clayton was there as usual or that he stayed far away from me the whole time.

Anyway, I managed to keep up my little nonchalant act for a full week following the breakup. It wasn't easy, and by the next youth group, where Clayton was conspicuously absent, I grew thoroughly tired of the whole charade. However, I kept it up. A big part of being a type A is pride — caring too much about my image and what others think of me. It's a hard act to keep up.

But now it's another Monday morning, the start of my second week without Clayton, and I'm sick of faking it. In fact, I am considering going to Clayton, taking the blame, and apologizing for the whole stupid mess. It will be humiliating, but I think I can do it. I am ready to beg him to come back to me.

If I do it soon enough, like today, we might even be able to make it to the Winter Ball next week. The only problem is, I'll have to swallow my great big pride. The mere thought makes the lump in my throat feel bigger than ever this morning.

"Are you okay?" Mary Beth asks as we're going up the front steps to Magnolia Park High School.

"Sure," I say in a blasé tone. "I'm just great."

She frowns at me. "You don't sound just great."

Now I look directly at her, feeling hot tears stinging my eyelids. "You're right," I confess, "I'm not."

Mary Beth reaches over, takes me by the arm, and leads me back down the steps to a nearby bench where we both sit down. "Talk to me, GraceAnn," she says in that calm, quiet manner that makes her Mary Beth and my best friend.

Instead of talking to her, I just start crying. And really, I hate playing the drama queen and I'm just certain that other students are staring at me as they head in the front door. I imagine they're gossiping about how pathetic I am and how Clayton was smart to dump me.

"Is this about Clayton?" Mary Beth asks with gentle empathy.

I nod, digging in my bag for a tissue.

"So you weren't really taking it as well as it appeared."

I shake my head no and blow my nose.

"Well, it's only natural that you should be hurting, GraceAnn. You and Clayton were together for almost a year."

"I know." I choke back a sob. "And I — I miss him. I really, really miss him."

"It'll get easier with time," she assures me.

Now I remember how brokenhearted Mary Beth was last summer when Jackson broke up with her. They'd only been going together for a couple of months, but she went totally to pieces when he dumped her for Lucinda Marx. And although I tried to be understanding, I wonder now if I really was. I was caught up in my new job at the pharmacy. And I was probably wrapped up in what I thought was my perfect romance with Clayton. Suddenly I suspect that I wasn't terribly supportive or a very good best friend. And I don't even know how to tell her I'm sorry.

"I think it's healthy to cry. Just get it all out and try to move on."

I carry on for a bit, and then she pulls out a hairbrush and attempts to help my tangled mop of strawberry blonde hair, smoothing it out. I guess I forgot to brush it this morning. She even digs out my lip gloss and hands it to me. "A little damage control."

I smudge on some gloss and take in a shaky breath. "I should probably get to my trig class now."

She glances at her watch and stands. "We can talk more later."

I nod like this is a good idea, but as we hurry into the building, I suspect I will return to my "just fine" act again. Really, it's too painful to admit that it hurts this much or that I'm such a wimpy mess inside.

But if I thought my problems were bad before, they suddenly feel much, much worse. I'm heading for the math department when I see something that cuts me to the core. I spot Clayton leaning against the lockers with a dreamy-looking expression on his face—the kind of look he used to reserve just for me, but now he is looking at *someone else*.

I peer between the traffic of students to spy on a petite blonde girl. I'm pretty sure her name is Avery and she's a sophomore. She's very attractive. I think she came to youth group once. But right now she is looking up at Clayton like he is a god. And I feel sick.

I turn away, pretending not to notice. Not that Clayton is looking at me. No, it's obvious (that intimate little snapshot has been indelibly burned into my mind) that Clayton only has eyes for pretty little Avery now. And if I thought I was hurting before, it's as if I've been speared clean through now. Still, I try to act normal as I walk into my trig class.

*Focus on math*, I tell myself. *Do your work.*

Trigonometry has never been my strong suit, and if I want to keep my grade point average up and secure good scholarships—and most important, be accepted at Stanford—I need to ace this class. *Just focus.*

However, it's not until the release bell rings that I realize I've managed to space out for the past forty minutes. It's like I got sucked into some kind of time warp, and now math is over and it's time to go to AP History.

So goes my day, as I drift from one class to the next, feeling like I'm having an out-of-body experience until seventh period when Mary Beth jolts me back to reality in art. "Are you okay?" she asks with a worried expression.

I just nod, bouncing a charcoal pencil up and down like a teeter-totter between my fingers. "Sure." No way am I going to admit, not even to Mary Beth, that I am devastated by seeing Clayton and Avery together.

"You acted weird at lunch, and you kind of have this glazed look now. What's going on, GraceAnn?"

I give her a fake smile. "Nothing."

She points to the blank piece of drawing paper in front of me. "Then why haven't you drawn a single line?"

I look down at the white sheet and shrug. "I guess I'm just thinking . . . waiting for some inspiration."

"Okay . . ." Mary Beth turns her attention back to her own work. "If you say so."

To appease her, I attempt to sketch some lines, although I'm not sure what they're meant to be and they don't resemble the magazine photo of a broken-down fence and wildflowers I'd chosen as my "inspiration piece." In fact, they don't resemble anything . . . besides random lines.

Why did I let Mary Beth talk me into taking art this year? Everyone knows I don't have a creative bone in my body. "But it will be good for you," she had urged me last spring. "Art helps to develop other parts of your brain." Well, that sounded good at the time. I'm not so sure now.

As I drive us home, both Mary Beth and I are unusually quiet. Well, to be fair, Mary Beth is always on the quiet side; I'm the one who usually keeps the conversation going. So I suppose I'm the one who is unusually quiet.

"You're going to get over this," she assures me when I pull up in front of her house.

I nod, swallowing hard against the lump in my throat. I do not want to break down in front of her again. "I know."

"It just takes time. And I know you're not exactly a patient person, but you need to give yourself time to heal."

I turn and look at her, taking in her long, wavy dark hair, green eyes, freckles, and whimsical-looking smile, and I know she means well. But she so does not get it.

"Trust me, by Christmas you'll be over him."

Now I cry again.

"Oh, GraceAnn, I'm so sorry. I didn't mean to make you cry."

"It's okay." I'm searching the console for the packet of tissues I usually keep in my car. "It's not your fault."

"Well, maybe it's good," she says quietly. "Like I said, you need to let the tears out."

So now I confess how I spotted Clayton with Avery this morning. "And you should've seen the look in his eyes," I blurt out. "It was like he was totally smitten with her." I choke on a sob. "And it's only been a week — just a little more than a week."

She puts her hand on my arm. "I know; I saw them together on my way to lunch." She shakes her head. "Guys can be such jerks sometimes."

"And I'll bet Avery isn't even a Christian. Clayton always said he wouldn't date a non-Christian. He's changing."

Mary Beth shrugs. "Jackson used to say the same thing . . . and look at him now. He doesn't even go to youth group anymore."

"Well, did you notice Clayton wasn't at youth group last night?"

"I didn't want to mention it."

"Stupid guys! Maybe we're better off without them."

"Maybe . . ." But she sounds doubtful.

"Except that it would be nice to go to the Winter Ball." I sigh. "I really thought Clayton might change his mind . . . want to get back together . . . and take me. I already knew what dress I was going to get and everything."

Mary Beth doesn't respond to this. Of course, as far as I know, she has no hopes of going to the Winter Ball this year. And this just makes me feel worse. Like what kind of friend am I? Obsessing over myself and how I won't be going to a stupid dance, and all this time my best friend has been hurting and I've barely even noticed.

"Oh well." I try to make my voice sound light. "It's not the end of the world, is it?"

She gives me a brave smile. "No, it's not."

"And who knows, maybe we can round up a couple of unsuspecting guys to take us to the dance." I force a laugh as I realize how ridiculous that idea might be.

"It's less than two weeks away, GraceAnn. Where do you plan to dig up some *unsuspecting* guys?"

"You're probably right, but I sure wouldn't mind making Clayton jealous."

She seems unsure about this.

"Okay, he probably wouldn't even care. But it might be fun for us, Mary Beth. I mean, to go to the dance. And there must be *some* guys who would take us."

"Who?" She looks thoroughly bewildered now.

"I don't know, but I'll try to think of something . . . or some-one . . . or a couple of someones."

"Good luck with that." She opens the car door.

"I'll get back to you," I promise as she gets out.

She chuckles. "Can't wait to hear what you come up with."

But now I'm determined. How hard could it be to find a couple of nice guys to take a couple of nice girls to a dance? And hey, we can go dutch if we need to. As I drive home, I consider the unattached guys in our youth group. By the time I pull into the driveway, I realize that none of them will work. There are some very specific reasons they're "unattached."

I turn off the car engine and stare up at my house like I'm seeing it for the first time. It's my parents' pride and joy, but I guess I take it for granted. Sure, it's comfortable enough. But sometimes I'm embarrassed by how big and fancy and expensive it is. Especially in our small town of Magnolia Park. But I suppose it's the type of house you'd expect two doctors to own. Impressive. From the outside you see an immaculate yard, lots of stonework, and windows that go on and on and cost a small fortune to have cleaned.

I reach for my bag and sigh. People who know our family describe my parents as "successful" and no doubt they are. But

I would describe them as busy and unavailable. Dad is a popular plastic surgeon and Mom is an ER doctor at St. Mark's. They make plenty of money, but sometimes it almost seems they don't have room in their busy lives of working, traveling, entertaining . . . for their only child—me.

The payoff is that I don't go without. Mary Beth is always quick to point out that I am totally spoiled. And maybe I am. Besides my sweet Honda Civic, I have all the latest electronic gadgets and toys, my own credit cards, and what she considers a hefty allowance. What she doesn't always understand is that I pay a price for all the material goods that are so "generously" heaped upon me . . . not to mention what I would trade them for. But since Mary Beth is being raised by a single mom who works as a real estate receptionist and barely scrapes by, I can't complain around her. Still, there are plenty of times I wish I could switch places with her.

The other thing Mary Beth doesn't quite grasp is that all of this comes with another steep price tag: parental expectations. Because I've always been fairly academic and a high achiever (aka type A personality), my parents expect me to attend a "good" college and a "good" med school and follow in their successful footsteps. And most of the time, I'm good with that. But on days like today, I'm not so sure I can keep up. And sometimes I wonder, what's the point—and who am I doing it for? Right now I just want to slink off to my room, crawl into bed, and escape into a long and undisturbed sleep.

## CHAPTER 2

Somehow I bumble, stumble, and fumble through week two of being without Clayton. I keep up a strong front and manage to convince Mary Beth that my hunt for dance dates is on the upswing. But the truth is, I am way too picky . . . and I am still pining for Clayton.

"You should just give up on the Winter Ball," Mary Beth tells me as we're going into art class on Friday. "It's only a week away and I doubt any guys are going to be interested at this point."

"Interested in *what*?" Bryant Morris asks in a teasing tone. He's holding open the door to the art room.

As I pass by, he gives me a sideways glance with a twinkle in his eye, and I just shake my head. Bryant is what I would describe as a "bad boy." Not that he's in trouble exactly . . . more like he *looks* like trouble. He wears a beat-up motorcycle jacket with a silver chain hanging from his baggy pants. Besides that, he walks with a swagger. He's the kind of guy who will talk back to a teacher, good-naturedly of course, and he has no problem sneaking a cigarette when he thinks no teachers are looking. I've known Bryant since third grade, and despite his slightly-rough-around-the-edges image, he has a good heart. And he's attractive — in that bad-boy sort of way.

"Nothing you'd be interested in," I say lightly as I head for our table.

"Don't be so sure, Lowery." He follows us back. After we're seated, he places his palms on the table next to me and leans forward, holding his face just inches from mine. I can smell tobacco on him.

I make a mock laugh. "Trust me, Bryant, you are *not* interested in this."

"Come on," he urges me with playful eyes.

I exchange glances with Mary Beth and she looks worried.

"Okay," he says, "let me guess."

I just shrug. "Knock yourself out."

"You girls are looking for dates for the Christmas dance."

I'm sure my jaw drops, but he just grins.

*"GraceAnn,"* Mary Beth hisses at me.

"But I'm sure you girls think you're too good for someone like me." He stands up straight now and, with a slightly wounded expression, shoves his hands in his pockets. "So much for that Christian love I've heard you preaching about all these years. It's obvious that words are cheap." He turns and walks away.

Now I'm stunned. I do try to express my faith in words, but who knew someone like Bryant Morris was listening? I turn back to Mary Beth. "Can you believe that?"

Her eyes are wide.

"I ought to go over there and tell him I'd love to go to the dance with him." I laugh. "I wonder what he'd say to that. Can you imagine Bryant Morris agreeing to take me to the Winter Ball?"

She shakes her head and looks even more astonished as she opens her portfolio.

So I stand and slowly wander over to where he's sitting with his best friend, Jorge Mendez. "I'm calling your bluff," I coolly tell Bryant. "You want to take me to the Winter Ball?"

He looks slightly stunned. Standing, he pushes his shaggy brown hair off his forehead, and his jacket cuff slips up high enough to reveal the edge of a tattoo. Now I'm not fond of tattoos, but I've seen it before and as tattoos go, it's not so bad. As I recall, it's some kind of a bird or a winged dragon. Still, I don't get how anyone could endure that kind of pain — and then be stuck with a permanent image like that. What if he changes his mind?

"Sure . . ." He makes a crooked grin. "You want to go with me?"

"Seriously?" Suddenly I'm second-guessing myself. What am I getting into?

"Oh, so now you're backing down?" His mouth twists to one side. "I figured you'd wimp out — "

"You're on," I say in a slightly smug tone. "It's a formal dance, which means a tux or suit for you, plus it's customary to take your date to a nice dinner beforehand." I pause. "And oh yeah, some guys even spring for a limo and dessert afterward."

Bryant nods with a sober expression, then quietly says, "Okay."

"Okay?" I blink and step back. "Meaning what?"

He grins. "Meaning it's a date, Lowery."

Now I'm too dumbfounded to respond.

"Unless you're backing out already?" He studies me. "Are you chicken?"

"No. Why should I be?" I'm trying to think of a graceful escape, a polite excuse, a way out of this. And did he not get what I just told him? That it is expensive?

"Good, then it's a date, *right*?" He says this like it's a

challenge, like he's tossing down the gauntlet or something.

"One more thing," I say quickly. "No alcohol."

He laughs. "Yeah, I kinda knew that from the start, Lowery."

"And quit calling me Lowery."

"Sure. So it's a date then?" He eyes me closely.

Now I'm feeling nervous. What have I gotten myself into? And suddenly I remember Mary Beth. She's my ace in the hole. "Well, it would be . . . except I promised Mary Beth that I wouldn't go without her, and it would be wrong to —"

"Jorge can take her." He pokes his friend in the shoulder. "Right, Jorge?"

Jorge looks slightly blindsided but nods. "Sure, I can take Mary Beth to the dance."

"But I —"

"Aha." Bryant points a finger at me. "So you *are* backing out. I knew you would."

"I am *not*. I'm just surprised . . . that's all."

"Then it's a date. You and me and Mary Beth and Jorge?"

I swallow hard, trying to think of something else. How do I hit rewind?

"Or maybe I was right about you and your Christian claims to love everyone. Like I said, talk is cheap, Lowery."

I point my finger back at him. "I already told you to quit calling me by my last name."

He nods. "Fine. *GraceAnn*."

"Next of all, do you fully comprehend that it's expensive to go to this dance? There are tickets and —"

"Yeah, yeah, you already told me all that, Lower — I mean, *GraceAnn*. I'm not an idiot."

"Also there's Mary Beth to consider. I need to run this past her."

"Why don't you let Jorge run it past her?" Bryant suggests.

And just like that, Jorge is on his way over to Mary Beth. I watch her face growing red and her flustered response, which I can't read from here, and then Jorge returns with a triumphant look.

"She said yes."

"*Really?*" I cannot believe it. "Well, okay then. If Mary Beth agrees, it looks like we have a date."

Bryant is grinning from ear to ear, and Mr. Faulkner is telling the class to take their seats and get to work, so I head back to our table. "Did you really tell Jorge yes?" I whisper to Mary Beth.

"I was so shocked," she sputters. "I didn't know what to say. And he looked so hopeful. And I actually like him — I mean, as a friend — and then he told me you agreed to go with Bryant if I agreed to go with him. So I just said sure, why not." She winces like she's in pain. "What are we going to do, GraceAnn?"

I glance over to where Bryant and Jorge are working on their projects and chatting quietly. "I guess we're going to go with them."

"What will people say?"

I shrug. "Why should we care?" See, there I go trying to be a type B personality when I feel like a nervous wreck inside.

"Right . . . why should we?" She still looks unsure.

"Besides, as Bryant pointed out, maybe it's our way to show them Christian love."

"So we're like missionaries?" Mary Beth's brow creases.

"Maybe so. We'll evangelize the whole night through."

"By the end of the dance, they'll probably be sick of us."

"And if they're not sick of us," I chuckle, "we'll get them to go to youth group on Sunday. And by the end of the night, we'll have them down on their knees repeating the Sinner's Prayer with Pastor Arnold."

That makes us start giggling like middle-school girls. And then we move on to a happier topic—discussing what we'll wear and making plans to go shopping this week. Is this a crazy idea? Well, of course. But for some reason I'm not too troubled by the idea of going to the Winter Ball with Bryant and Jorge. In fact, I'm a little curious as to the reaction we'll get. Maybe Clayton will think I've changed, or at the least think I'm taking some risks by hanging with the bad boys. Whatever the case, I'm sure tongues will wag. And as out of character as it seems, I'm not terribly concerned. Not yet anyway.

More disturbing—and something I'm trying not to obsess over—is that my lack of attention in my classes these past two weeks has put a couple of my previously good grades in serious limbo. And I'm not quite sure how I will get them back . . . or how they will impact my close-to-perfect GPA . . . or how disappointed my parents will be when they find out. Still, I'm trying not to think about it, and I certainly don't plan to mention anything to my parents.

Not that they have time to listen. On Friday night they go to a party with friends. On Saturday morning they sleep in.

But I get up bright and early, and after a bowl of cereal, I arrive like clockwork at Lowery's Drugstore. Nine o'clock sharp.

"On time again," Uncle Russ says. He's my dad's brother—the "med-school dropout and underachiever," according to Dad. But I know Uncle Russ worked hard to get his degree, and he seems perfectly happy to me. He enjoys visiting with customers, measuring pills, and filling prescriptions. He even whistles when he sweeps the sidewalk outside the pharmacy. He takes pride in the business he and Aunt Lindsey have owned for as long as I can remember.

And I am perfectly happy to work for them. It's not that I really need the money, but I like having my own job and responsibilities. I like that my aunt and uncle appreciate me and aren't afraid to tell me so. And it makes me feel independent to come to work. I also think it will look good on my résumé someday when I need to get a real job. So far I've learned how to write out orders, ring up sales, check in merchandise, and clean the bathroom.

"How would you feel about making a delivery?" Aunt Lindsey asks me after I return from my lunch break.

"Sure, why not?"

"It's Miss Julia," she tells me.

"Miss Julia?" Now I'm worried because Miss Julia is one of my favorite people. She goes to our church and is also a regular customer here. Whenever she comes in, she lingers to chat with me, and I just thoroughly enjoy her. Despite being in her eighties, she walks to the pharmacy to get what she needs and is always cheerful and bright. "Is she sick?"

"Yes. Poor thing has shingles and it's making her miserable." Then my aunt explains that shingles is a virus related to chicken pox. "It attacks your nerve endings and can be extremely painful and debilitating." She hands me a little white sack and an address. "Here's what her doctor called in for her."

As I drive to Miss Julia's house, which is only a few blocks away, I wonder what it would feel like to be in my eighties . . . and to be sick. I can't even imagine. She lives in this quaintly old-fashioned neighborhood not far from the high school, but her yard and house look a little run-down and neglected. Even for December. I ring the doorbell, knock on the door, and after several minutes Miss Julia appears looking faded and pale and wearing a worn yellow bathrobe.

"Come in, come in," she says in a weak voice.

I follow her into the dimly lit house and into a cluttered living room. It smells a little musty in here, and a slightly scraggly orange cat is curled up in an easy chair. Miss Julia eases herself down into a pink recliner and lets out a weary sigh. "Oh my . . . someone should just get out a gun and shoot me."

"What?" I stare at her.

"Put me out of my misery," she mutters.

"Oh, Miss Julia." I sit on the sofa across from her. "You must feel really terrible."

"I do . . . I most certainly do." She looks at me with frightened eyes. "It's not fun getting old . . . and being alone."

I hold out the bag. "I brought your medicine. Maybe you'll feel better if you take some."

But she just sighs.

"How about if I get you some water?"

She waves her hand. "Water makes me sick to my stomach."

I think hard. "Milk then?"

She just shakes her head.

"Well, I'll look for something." I find my way to the kitchen, which is even more cluttered than the living room, and pull out my cell phone to make a quick call to the pharmacy, explaining the situation to my aunt.

"Find something soft in the fridge," she tells me. "Like yogurt or applesauce. Then have her eat that with the pills. And those pain pills will probably take effect quickly and help her to sleep, so make sure she's in a comfortable place."

So I scavenge through the fridge, finding a little carton of strawberry yogurt, which thankfully is not past its expiration date. Then I get a spoon and return to Miss Julia. "My aunt says to take the pills with yogurt." I pop open the top and stick in the spoon. It takes a bit of coaxing and patience, but eventually she gets the pills down, then leans back as if she's exhausted.

"Why don't you put your feet up?" I ease her chair into the reclining position. She moans in pain. "I'm sorry, but my aunt says these pills will help you to rest."

"I haven't slept in days," she says wearily. "I'm afraid I may never sleep again."

I find a knitted blanket and lay it over her. "Well, maybe you'll sleep now. Just close your eyes and try to relax."

"You won't leave yet, will you?" She looks frightened.

"I'll wait until you go to sleep."

"Thank you." She leans her head back and closes her eyes, but her mouth still looks tight with pain.

I call the pharmacy again, explain her request, and Aunt Lindsey urges me to stick around. To kill time, I decide to straighten up a bit. I suspect her illness has made it difficult to keep things picked up.

After about an hour, I notice two things: Miss Julia is sleeping soundly and her house is much tidier. I leave her a little note, telling her to call the pharmacy if she has any problems or needs any help, and then I quietly let myself out.

As I drive back to the pharmacy, I pray for her to get better. And I realize that my life's problems aren't such a big deal compared to hers. She is all alone and sick and maybe even frightened. I make a decision to come visit with her next week . . . just to make sure she's doing okay.

With winter break around the corner and finals week lurking, I'm growing increasingly concerned about my grades. I thought I'd get a handle on the situation and have it all fixed by now, but on Monday morning when I find out I scored an F on my last trig test, I'm in complete and absolute shock. An F? I feel sick inside and I cannot believe it. How could I have sunk so low so fast? Seriously, what is happening to me? It doesn't help matters when I remember I got a D last week. I thought that was just a fluke, but now I have to admit that I'm floundering here.

"I really need to buckle down and study this week," I grumble to Mary Beth at lunch.

"Don't we all."

"No," I insist. "I'm serious. I'm in trouble." And although it's humiliating, I confide to her about my bad grade.

"No way!" She looks nearly as shocked as I feel.

"Way . . ." I let out a hopeless sigh as I unwrap my straw. "I feel like I'm slipping into a black hole. Going down."

"Wow, that's tough." She pours dressing on her salad. "I mean, I've pulled a couple of Ds before, but this is you, GraceAnn. You're the academic."

"You know what was weird?" I shove the straw into my drink. "I got an F, but I went over the test carefully and I actually got more than half of the answers correct. And the ones I missed were actually close. How does that equal an F?"

"Is it because of the curve?"

Admittedly, I'm not familiar with low grades, but this still makes no sense. "I thought Fs were for students who got most of the answers wrong . . . because they didn't study."

"Maybe that's true in some classes . . . like the ones I take." She gives me a sympathetic half smile. "But you take the hard classes, GraceAnn. Maybe the curve is sharper in there."

Okay, I know all about the curve and how it works, but I never concerned myself with it . . . because I'm usually on the *good* side of the curve. "You mean because the students in the hard classes are *smarter*?"

"There's that too," she says quietly.

"Too?" I peer curiously at her. "Meaning?"

She glances around to see if anyone is listening to us. "Meaning the curve probably gets skewed because so many kids cheat."

"You really think so?"

She nods in a sad way. "I know so."

"How do you know?"

"I've seen them, GraceAnn. With my own eyes, I've *seen* them."

"You're kidding? You've actually seen people cheating?"

"Keep your voice down." She gives me a warning look.

"Why?" I look around.

"Because this is a dangerous subject."

"What are you talking about?" Suddenly I'm curious as to how my best friend is an expert on cheating. "Dangerous how?"

"Dangerous in that some kids take it very seriously. I've heard it's a big business."

"That's crazy." Now I try to remember the times I've been taking tests . . . if I've ever observed anything suspicious. "I've never seen it happen. I know I would remember that."

"I've seen you during an exam. You get so focused on your own test that you're oblivious to everyone else."

I nod. "I suppose that's true."

"And that's just because you're always obsessed with doing your best."

"And you're not?"

She shrugs. "I try . . . I just don't obsess. I'm okay with average grades."

"Your grades are better than average."

"Maybe. But I don't take the kinds of classes you do."

I let out a long sigh. "Now I'm wishing I didn't either."

After lunch, in AP Biology, I feel like I'm experiencing déjà vu when I get the results from last Friday's test only to discover I got a D minus. This is bad. Really bad. But as I look over my answers on the quiz, I realize that once again I got most of them right. And yet I received a D minus for my effort. How is that fair? Yes, I know . . . the curve. But even so, it seems so wrong. And now I'm really wondering about what Mary Beth said—what if everyone really is cheating?

I glance over at Kelsey Nelson, who is sitting across from me. I'm still trying to wrap my head around this girl . . . wondering when she turned into such an academic. Because I remember when she had serious trouble with her multiplication tables back in fifth grade. Anyway, I'm trying to be discreet, but I want to get a peek at her test grade. Finally she lifts her hand to push a strand of hair away from her face, and I see she received an A. *An A!*

I try not to let my astonishment show, but I'm in shock. Kelsey getting an A is as stunning as me getting a D minus, and I wonder how Ms. Bannister doesn't scratch her head over this one. But as usual, Ms. Bannister has her head partly in a book as she starts up PowerPoint and is obviously preparing for a lecture.

I glance back at Kelsey, and I've got to admit that she's nice enough and, despite being a cheerleader, not stuck up at all. But, no offense intended, if you looked up the definition of *dumb blonde* in the dictionary, I'm pretty sure her picture would be next to it.

Okay, that's a bit harsh. But seriously, the girl has never been a brainiac. I was more than a little stunned to see she was taking AP Biology this year. Still, it's not my job to judge her, and to be honest, I thought she'd help push the bell curve grading system in my direction anyway. Apparently I was wrong. Dead wrong.

I'm still mystified by this as I attempt to focus on Ms. Bannister's lecture. By the end of the period, I feel almost certain that Kelsey must be one of those that Mary Beth mentioned—a *cheater*. And yet I've never seen anything to prove this new theory. Of course, as Mary Beth pointed out, I've never been looking either.

But the idea that someone like Kelsey might be cheating, might be changing the whole grading system for everyone in this class—especially me—well, it just totally irks me. Seriously, I am livid. Not only that, but if what Mary Beth says is true, Kelsey is probably not the only one doing this. It is so wrong!

By art class at the end of the day, I'm still fuming. I try not to show it, but I am so enraged. The more I think about it, the angrier I get. Today Bryant and Jorge have moved to our table. I suppose they think if they're taking us to the dance on Saturday, it buys them the right to sit with us. And really, I don't mind. I just don't want to talk to anyone.

"What's eating you?" Bryant asks me toward the end of class.

"Huh?" I look up from where I've been staring blankly at my drawing.

He points to the paper in front of me, and Mary Beth looks uncomfortable for me. She probably thinks I'm moping over Clayton again, and I suppose on some levels I am, but this cheating thing is what's really got me frustrated. I look at Bryant's face. Is he one of them? Is he a cheater? And if he is, do I still want to go to the dance with him? I don't think so.

"If you really must know," I begin slowly, trying not to sound like I'm seething although I clearly am, "I'm obsessing over the fact that there are kids in this school who think it's acceptable to cheat." I lock gazes with him in a challenging way.

Bryant simply laughs. "You mean you just figured that out, Lowery?"

I nod indignantly.

"She got an F in math."

I toss Mary Beth a warning look.

"Ouch." Bryant seems truly sympathetic. "That's gotta hurt. Especially for a brainiac like you."

"And I got a D minus in AP Biology," I confess bitterly.

"You take AP Biology?" Jorge looks impressed.

"And Kelsey Nelson got an A," I continue hopelessly.

"Uh-oh." Mary Beth looks concerned now, like I'm saying too much. But I don't care.

"So what are you saying?"

"What do you think I'm saying, Jorge?" I toss back. "Tell me, how does someone like Kelsey Nelson suddenly turn into an A student? Especially in AP Biology?"

"She studied?" He gives an apologetic grin.

"Yeah, right." I roll my eyes.

"You think Kelsey Nelson cheats?" Bryant asks quietly.

"Duh . . ."

"Did you *see* her cheat?" Bryant asks me.

I shake my head. "No. It's just a theory."

"I've seen people cheating." Jorge uses a hushed tone. "Lots of times."

"Why didn't you tell someone?" I demand.

His dark eyes get wide. "Are you kidding?"

"Why not?" I turn to Mary Beth now. "And how about you? You said the same thing—that you've seen students cheating, but you don't tell. *Why not?*"

Mary Beth bites her lip, and I can tell the idea of ratting on someone is terrifying to her.

I look at Bryant. "I suppose you agree with them?"

He just shrugs.

"I just don't get it. I mean, it's so unfair. Cheaters ruin the grading system for the rest of us." I look at Bryant and Jorge. "Do you guys cheat?"

Bryant chuckles. "If I did, do you think I'd tell you?"

I consider this.

"And Jorge doesn't need to." He grins at his friend.

"Really?" Mary Beth looks interested.

"Jorge doesn't like anyone to know, but he's got a seriously high GPA," Bryant says.

"It's nothing, man." Jorge turns red.

Now the release bell rings, and we're gathering up our stuff and getting ready to leave, but I'm still fuming. Bryant and Jorge make small talk as we head out, and Mary Beth reminds me that we planned to do some shopping today . . . for the Winter

Ball. Although I was enthusiastic before, I couldn't care less now. As a result of my dismal test grades, my heart is just not in it. However, I see the hopeful look in her eyes, and I don't want to let her down. So we bid the guys adieu and I brace myself for shopping.

"You'll bring your grades back up," Mary Beth assures me as I silently drive us toward the mall. "You always do."

"I don't know . . ."

"I know. You're such an academic, GraceAnn. No way will you let these past couple of weeks bring you down. By winter break your grades will be stellar."

"I hope you're right." But as I'm turning into the mall parking lot, I'm not so sure. For some reason I feel like I'm standing on the edge of that "slippery slope" that our youth pastor warns us about from time to time. Not that I've done anything wrong exactly—well, besides not studying enough. And really, that wasn't intentional. But even so, it feels like my feet are unsteady beneath me . . . like one misstep and I could tumble downward.

However, as we go inside the formal wear store, I figure that I'm just obsessing. As usual. *Lighten up*, I tell myself as we start looking at dresses. Mary Beth is right. I'll work hard and pull my grades out of the toilet, and by Christmas this grim scenario will be nothing more than an unpleasant memory.

"I have a feeling I'll need to do my shopping at Déjà Vu," Mary Beth tells me after we've perused several dress racks. "Most of these are out of my price range."

"What do you think of this one?" I hold up a red satin dress. "It's kind of like what I imagined I'd wear if I went with Clayton." I frown, wishing I could get that boy out of my brain.

She frowns and shakes her head. "No offense, GraceAnn, but it looks kind of trampy."

"Trampy?" I walk over to where I can hold it up in front of the mirror and see it more clearly. It's not that I don't trust Mary Beth's taste, but she leans way toward the conservative side. I study the fitted red dress carefully, imagining how it would look. "I think it looks quite festive. And Christmassy. And this color reminds me of cranberry sauce." I turn to look at her. "You really think it looks trampy?"

"Go ahead and try it on if you want," she tells me. But her expression says this is a waste of time. Even so, I pick out several sizes of the same style and carry them back to the dressing room. After a couple of tries, I find the one that fits best and step out of the changing room to show her. "What do you think now?" I twirl around in front of the three-way mirror.

"Well, it does fit you nicely." But she still looks unsure.

I stop and look more closely, gather up my hair in an upsweep do, and strike a pose. I imagine myself in a great pair of shoes and some sparkly faux diamonds and think I'll look like a million bucks—and I might even turn Clayton's head. "Well, I *love* it!"

"But I thought we were going to wear *long* dresses," she says in a disappointed tone.

I shrug. "From what I've heard around school, most of the girls are going with cocktail dresses for this dance."

"Does that mean you plan to *drink* cocktails too?" She scowls at me.

"No, of course not." I laugh. "And don't worry, you can wear a long dress if you want to—it's not like there are rules about this stuff."

"No . . . if you're getting that, I'll try to find something that works with it."

"You should just get what you like," I tell her. "What you feel comfortable in."

"Well, you know I don't like showing my legs—"

"You have great legs, Mary Beth. I don't see why you wouldn't—"

"I have enormous calves and you know it!"

"That's how *you* see it. I think your legs are very shapely." I give her a sly look. "And I have a feeling Jorge would agree."

She rolls her eyes. "Please, don't remind me. I still can't believe we agreed to go out with those two gangsters."

"Gangsters?" I let out a hoot. "Bryant and Jorge are not gangsters, Mary Beth. They just walk to a different drummer. And the more I get to know them, the more I like them both."

"Maybe, but I'll bet we are the laughingstock of youth group by Sunday night."

"We'll just tell them we're evangelizing."

"Yeah . . . right."

Okay, I'm not as confident about this as I sound. But I am glad I'm going to the dance, glad I'm going to look hot in this dress, and I'm hoping Clayton will be pea green with envy when he sees me laughing and dancing with Bryant Morris. It will serve him right!

## CHAPTER 4

L ater in the week, I'm relieved to see that Mary Beth hit the jackpot at the thrift store. "That is gorgeous," I tell her as she models a vintage cocktail dress in a deep forest green. "It's beautiful with your green eyes."

"You don't think we'll look too Christmassy with you in red and me in green?"

"I think we'll look like knockouts," I assure her.

"And check out these shoes." She holds up a sweet pair of black velvet wedges. "I got them at that new discount shoe store."

"Perfect."

"Did you get your shoes yet?"

I confess that I haven't.

"Then you need to check out the discount store," she urges me. "They have everything."

So we agree to go there after school. But as I'm driving, all I can think about is how my grades in trig and AP Biology have still not recovered and, at this rate, there is no way my GPA won't be impacted.

"You're awfully quiet," Mary Beth points out as I park in front of the shoe store.

I shrug and turn off the engine. "Sorry."

"Are you thinking about Clayton again?"

I want to tell her that's it, but I don't want to lie. "I'm obsessing over my grades again," I confess as we get out. "They're not getting any better."

"Oh . . ." She nods sympathetically. "I'm sorry."

"I don't know what to do."

She pats me on the back. "I know what you'll do, GraceAnn."

I look hopefully at her. "What?"

"You'll study hard and pull As on all your finals and your grades will improve."

I frown. "I'm not so sure."

She gives me a confident smile. "Maybe I know you better than you know yourself."

I force a smile. "I hope so."

For a while, I distract myself with shoe shopping, but in the back of my mind, I'm still obsessing over two things: (1) that my grades are in the toilet and (2) that some kids are cheating and getting away with it.

"Just three days until the big night," Mary Beth reminds me as I drop her at her house. "Can we get ready at your house?"

"Sure. That'd be cool."

"You know, GraceAnn, all things considered . . . I mean, how we both lost our boyfriends . . . I can't believe how happy I am that we decided to do this." She gives me a bright smile. "Thanks for pushing me."

I smile back. "Sure."

"And don't worry so much about your grades. You'll pull them up by the end of the term."

I nod, hoping she's right. But at the moment, all I can think about is that I have two exams tomorrow and I know I need to cram for them. Even if I have to stay up all night, I will do everything it takes to ace them.

"How's life?" Dad asks me as I come in the house. Rory jumps up, putting his paws on my thighs and wagging his tail ecstatically.

I give Dad a weak smile and scratch Rory's ear. "Okay."

Now Dad looks curious. "Just *okay?*"

So I hold up my bag, pretending to be happy. "No, Dad, I'm better than okay. I just got a cool pair of shoes for less than twenty bucks. Can you believe it?"

He grins. "Hey, I like the sound of that."

"Where's Mom?" I gently push Rory down.

"She's working late. Another ER doctor came down with the flu."

"Oh."

"I heated up some lasagna." He nods toward the kitchen. "If you want some, it's still in the oven. I already ate."

"Thanks. I'll take it to my room. I'm cramming tonight."

"Finals already?"

I shrug. "Just some weekly tests. Finals are next week."

He pats me on the head, just like he used to do when I was little. "I'm so proud of you, GraceAnn. You'll probably surpass both your parents academically."

I want to tell him not to hold his breath, but instead I smile.

"I bet we'll start hearing back from some of the colleges before long," he says as he follows me and Rory to the kitchen. "Kids like you usually get early acceptance letters."

I set my bag on a bar stool and peel off my jacket, trying to think of a response to that. I want to ask him whether an early acceptance will be affected by a drop in my GPA, but I'm pretty sure I can guess the answer to that one. "Smells good," I say as I open the oven door.

"Your mom and I felt lucky to make it into USC," he tells me, not for the first time, "but we'll be so proud if you go to Stanford, GraceAnn."

I just nod as I cut into the lasagna. It's the frozen kind but still pretty tasty.

"And we'll be even prouder if one of the Ivy Leagues comes calling for you." Now he starts telling me about a doctor friend whose son is going to Harvard. I've heard the story before, and I used to like it. Now it makes me feel slightly sick.

"Well, if I'm going to make it into Harvard, I better hit the books."

He chuckles. "A girl after my own heart."

With Rory on my heels, I take my lasagna to my room and get comfortable. Rory settles beneath my desk, and as I fork into my food, I start poring over the information I need to absorb before tomorrow. But it's weird, like my brain isn't functioning properly . . . like something isn't quite working. Even so, I press on, studying and reading and forcing myself to stay awake until nearly two in the morning when I hear Mom coming into the house.

Not wanting to draw her attention, I snap off the light and remain quiet until I can hear that she's gone to bed. Then I study some more. Rory, tired of waiting for me, hops onto my bed, looking hopefully at me. But I keep going and going until my eyes refuse to stay open anymore.

· · · · · · · · · ·

When morning comes, I feel blurry eyed and fuzzy headed. Dad has already left for work, probably has an early morning surgery scheduled. And Mom, I'm guessing, is still sleeping. I fill a travel mug with coffee and carry it to the car with me. With no time to spare, I drive a little fast to Mary Beth's, where she is waiting a bit impatiently.

"I thought you forgot me." She jumps into the passenger seat. "I tried to call, but your phone was off."

"Yeah, it's probably dead," I say as I take off. "Sorry to be late."

"Wow, you look . . . uh, well, not so good."

"Thanks a lot." I glance at my image in the rearview mirror as I wait for the light to turn. There are dark shadows beneath my eyes and my skin looks a little pasty.

"Did you pull an all-nighter studying?"

I nod and take off with a jerk, spilling coffee down the front of my jacket.

"Here, let me help." She reaches in the console for some tissues, attempting to blot me off as I drive. Then she smoothes over my hair. "No time for a hairbrush either?"

I shrug.

As I drive, Mary Beth helps to straighten me up a little. "Am I presentable now?" I ask as we get out of the car.

"Here." She hands me her lip gloss. "This might help."

"Thanks." I smear some on, then hear what must be the late bell ringing. "We better run." I hand it back. "Sorry about being late."

"It's okay," she says as we start jogging. "I know you hate being late way more than I do."

This is true. Very true. But to make matters worse, it's trigonometry I'm late for and Mr. VanDorssen hates that. When I slip in the door, he's already handing out the weekly exam. I take my seat and focus on my paper, but as I work to complete it, I feel distracted by two things: (1) my own inability to think clearly and (2) my curiosity over whether anyone is cheating. I glance furtively around, spying on other students. So much so that I garner a suspicious look from Mr. VanDorssen — and that makes me feel guilty.

I turn my eyes back to my own paper and force myself to plod through the problems. *You're probably doing better than it feels like.* That's usually the case with me. Even so, I feel uncertain as I hand it in. I have the distinct feeling that I am only going to fall further and further behind.

As the morning progresses, this feeling persists. And by lunchtime I'm questioning why I ever signed up for classes like trig and AP History and third-year Spanish and AP English — and all in the morning too. What was I thinking? And I still have AP Biology (and that test) to go.

"Are you okay?" Mary Beth peers at me as we sit at the lunch table.

I shrug. "Besides being exhausted and feeling dumber than a post?"

"Oh, GraceAnn." She shakes her head. "You're so hard on yourself."

"For good reason." I tell her how I'm sure I blew my trig test.

"You probably aced it. Remember how many times you've felt just like this and everything turned out fine?"

I try to absorb this. She could be right. I've been known to freak over how badly I've done only to find out I did just fine. But by AP Biology, I'm thinking differently. I thought I studied hard for this test, but as I sit there poring over the multiple-choice questions, I feel like I never opened an AP Biology book in my life. Like I should just wad up the test, hand it to Ms. Bannister, and tell her I'm going to swap this class for an easier one . . . like pottery, perhaps.

Just when I feel like giving up, I glance up and notice Kelsey looking calm and collected as she carefully pens in an answer. Feeling guilty for looking in her direction, I quickly divert my eyes back to my own paper, hunkering down as if I'm thinking hard. But while I'm hunkered there, I glance back at Kelsey, watching her through my half-closed eyes filtered by my eyelashes—and that's when I see it!

For some reason, I notice Kelsey has a thin slip of paper around her wrist. It's tucked neatly beneath the cuff of her black-and-gold cheerleader jacket. (And it occurs to me that it's a bit warm in here for a heavy jacket like that.) Anyway, the strip of yellow paper could almost be mistaken for a bracelet, but from where I'm sitting, I can see that it's not and I can see that this "bracelet" has Kelsey's full attention too.

As if she's scratching an itch, she uses her other hand to flip the paper "bracelet" ever so slightly, making it turn. Then she reaches up to scratch her nose, almost as if to camouflage the other movement. I can't really tell from here, but I suspect there is writing on the inside of this clever little bracelet and she's adjusted it to see the answer to the next question. And I'm sure my jaw is dropping as I stare at this phenomenon.

That's when I hear Ms. Bannister clearing her throat from up in front, and I glance up there to find her looking directly at me now . . . almost as if she's suspicious of what I'm doing. She cocks her head slightly to one side with a creased forehead. Seriously, does she suspect that I'm cheating? Trying to copy off Kelsey's paper?

Feeling my cheeks flush, I look back down at my own exam and force myself to reread the last question . . . and then I force myself to answer it the best I can. Fueled by frustration and anger, I continue like this through the test. I skip the questions

I'm unsure about and answer the ones I think I know. Then I go back and attempt to make some "educated" guesses for the ones I skipped.

My dad taught me this process long ago — a way to eliminate options in multiple-choice questions to help you arrive at the likeliest possible answers. Finally, the release bell rings, and I know that although I probably flunked this test, I have to turn it in.

To my surprise (although I don't know why I'm the least bit surprised), Kelsey has already turned in her test and is merrily going on her way. Feeling flustered and foolish, I hand Ms. Bannister my dog-eared test, then take off to follow Kelsey. No way am I letting her get away with this. Thanks to that black-and-gold cheerleader outfit, the petite blonde is easy to spot.

I catch up with her just as she's heading into the girls' restroom, probably on her way to flush the evidence, but I duck in behind her, grab her by the arm, and glare down into her startled blue eyes.

"Just a minute," I say sharply. And with a kind of nerve I've never experienced before, I yank up her jacket sleeve, grab the paper bracelet from her wrist, and snatch it off, shoving it in her face.

"What are you — ?"

"You cheated!"

With big eyes, Kelsey looks desperately around the room to see if anyone is here to witness the spectacle, but it seems to be just the two of us. "Please," she says urgently, "give that back to me."

I shove the bracelet down deep into my jeans pocket and shake my head. "No. I'm going to go tell Ms. Bannister. Right now."

"Please, GraceAnn." She grabs my arms with both hands. "Please, don't tell. I'm begging you. *Please!*"

I stare at her in disbelief. "There's no way I'm not telling. Your cheating is ruining my grades and everyone else's —"

"Everyone else in the class is cheating. Are you going to rat on all of them too?"

"Not *everyone* cheats."

She makes a little laugh and releases my arms. "That just shows what you don't know."

I firmly shake my head. "I don't cheat."

"Yes." She looks at me with what almost seems like admiration. "But that's because you're brilliant. You always have been, GraceAnn. But not everyone can be as smart as you."

Now another girl comes into the restroom and Kelsey points at me. "I'm serious," she says in a chirpy voice. "I just love that sweater on you, GraceAnn. It's so your color."

Caught off guard, I look down at my dark brown pullover and frown.

"I mean, it matches your eyes." She nods to where the girl is going into the stall. "Such a nice chocolate brown."

"Uh . . . well, thanks."

"And I'd love to chat with you some more, but I'm running late for cheerleading class. Want to walk together?"

"Uh, sure, I guess so." So now we're walking and talking, and Kelsey, while keeping on her cheerleader happy face, is begging me to keep quiet. "You've heard about the zero-tolerance rule," she says as we turn toward the PE department. "If you rat me out, I'll get suspended and I'll be off the cheerleading squad and —"

"You should've thought of that sooner."

"And my parents will kill me. You don't know my stepdad,

GraceAnn. He's unbelievable when it comes to this kind of stuff. I'm sure your parents are understanding and nice. But my stepdad is a monster." She frowns. "It's his fault I even took AP Biology."

"Why's that?"

"He challenged me. He said I was too stupid."

"That's a little harsh."

"Well, you don't know him." Now she looks at me with teary eyes. "Please, don't tell on me. Honestly, my life is over if you rat me out. Without cheerleading, I might as well go jump off a bridge or something."

Okay, now I feel guilty and a bit like an ogre.

We're close to the gym now and she pulls me down a quiet corridor away from curious onlookers. "Really, I don't know what I'd do if I got kicked off. I'm not academic like you. All I have is cheerleading, and if you take that away" —her voice cracks— "please, GraceAnn, I'm begging you. I'll do anything if you promise not to tell on me."

I consider this. Maybe I am overreacting . . . and not being very Christian. "Will you promise not to cheat anymore?"

She looks worried but then nods, holding up her hand. "I promise."

I roll my eyes. "Okay, I'll probably regret this, but fine. I won't tell . . . this time anyway. If it happens again—"

Kelsey throws her arms around me, giving me a big hug. "I always knew you were a nice girl, GraceAnn. Thank you! *Thank you!*"

I let out a long sigh. "You better keep your promise," I call out as she hurries toward the locker room. I pat the tiny lump where the bracelet is still in my jeans pocket and shake my head. I'll probably be sorry.

But as I head toward my next class, I realize that I'm already sorry. Not about Kelsey—at least not too much—but about the way I blew my AP Biology test just now. I know it's going to earn me another D minus . . . perhaps even an F. And I still have finals next week, my only chance at raising that grade, and I've got two seriously bad test grades to contend with. Not to mention a couple less-than-stellar ones earlier, grades I'd felt sure I'd pull up by now.

Unless . . . A crazy thought goes through my head and I reach down and pat the little lump in my pocket. What would it hurt? What if I asked to retake today's test? And what if I did better? It could change my final grade.

Of course, this idea is followed by a boatload of guilt. How on earth could I possibly consider such a thing? Have I lost my mind? And yet Kelsey's words are still ringing in my ears: "Everyone in the class is cheating." Is that really true? And if it is true, how will I ever have a chance to pull up my grade? Even if I do my very best, how can I ever hope to compete? How can I possibly get anything more than just a satisfactory grade? And a C just won't cut it. It will lower my GPA, and it will do nothing to get me into Stanford. And how disappointed will my parents be if I can't meet their expectations?

With this in mind, perhaps combined with sleep deprivation and high anxiety, I find myself on my way to the science and math department at the beginning of seventh period. I shouldn't be skipping art like this, but my grade in there is not in peril. All you need to do in art is complete your projects and you're pretty much assured an A. Art and journalism are what I consider my *free-ride* classes. However, I know Mary Beth will be concerned at my absence, but I can explain it all to her later. Well, not *all* of it. I'm sure I'll never tell anyone *all* of what I'm about to do. In fact, I'm hoping I'll be able to erase it from my mind too. After I'm done.

## CHAPTER 5

"**G**raceAnn?" Ms. Bannister looks up from grading papers with a confused expression. "Did you forget something?"

"Sorry to disturb you," I say quickly, just as I rehearsed it on my way here. "But I thought this was your free period, and I hate to bother you but I know I did poorly on the test earlier." And suddenly I'm pouring out my heart, or hoping it sounds that way. I tell her about my recent breakup with Clayton and how it's messed with my study habits and how I didn't sleep last night. "As a result, I was just totally unfocused in class after lunch — and I blew the test."

She leans forward and peers curiously at me. "You do look a little under the weather. Do you think you might be coming down with that flu that's going around?"

"I'm not sure." Then I tell her how my mom works in the ER and some of the doctors have gotten it, which I'm sure is just another pity plea.

"Maybe you should go home."

"But I feel better now." I stand straighter. "Anyway, I'm wondering if there's any chance I can retake that test now?"

She studies me closely. "You mean the test you just took?"

"It was like my mind was all muddled then." I can't believe how easy it is for me to lie like this. "I studied a lot, but I was really distracted and frustrated." I glance around the quiet room. "But with everyone gone, I think I can do it." My heart is pounding so loudly; I'm surprised she can't hear it.

She presses her lips together, adjusts her glasses, then shrugs. "Okay. I guess I can let you retake it. This one time." She fishes an exam out of her briefcase and hands it to me, nodding up at the clock. "You better get on it. You only have about thirty minutes left and then I'm out of here."

With butterflies in my stomach, I hurry back to my usual spot and sit down, carefully placing my bag on the table on my left side, which provides a slight barricade to my left hand. Then I start working on the test. From time to time, I adjust the bracelet, which is securely around my wrist, flipping it around as needed to copy the answers. I feel a strange rush of nerves and excitement—a mixture of guilt and fear. Most of all, disbelief. Am I really doing this?

Almost more surprising is how easy it is to do this. And to my astonishment, Ms. Bannister never even gives me a second look as she continues marking papers. She has no idea that I'm cheating. Even so, I'm sure my blood pressure must be scary high, and my stomach twists and turns like a time bomb is ticking away down there. I just hope I don't throw up from all the adrenaline raging through me. I finish the test with ten minutes to spare, but I pretend to still be struggling through. I wait until the last minute before I go and give it to her.

"Was it worth it?" she asks.

I feel a jolt of shock—does she know what I did? That I cheated? But then I study her expression, and I can tell she's simply inquiring about the test.

So I nod firmly. "Yes, I'm sure it was. I felt so much more together just now." I make a forced smile. "Thanks for giving me a second chance."

She smiles back. "Well, I know you're a conscientious student, GraceAnn." Now her smile fades a bit. "And I was a little concerned that your grades were slipping. I hope you're back on track now."

"Me too." I thank her again, then hurry on out, and, without stopping, go straight to the same restroom that I confronted Kelsey in just an hour ago. With a pounding heart and a tossing stomach, I turn on the tap full blast and splash cold water on my flushed face. When I finally stop and look up into the mirror, I'm shocked at what I see. My pale face has splotchy red spots on it, the shadows beneath my eyes appear even darker, and my damp hair hangs around my face in messy clumps. I look sick. And I feel sicker than I look.

*What have I just done?*

Hearing someone coming in the door, I duck into a stall, then wait until the two chatty freshmen girls freshen up their makeup and leave. Then I go back out to assess the damage. My face is a little less flushed, but there is still a very guilty look in my dark eyes. It's as if the truth is written all over my face—GraceAnn is a CHEATER.

I dig in my bag for lip gloss and mascara and do my best to make my face look seminormal. I run a brush through my hair, fluff it a bit, then stand straighter. *You have to get it together.* I need to find Mary Beth and convince her that I'm just fine and that I haven't lost my mind. As for my morals . . . well, I don't plan to discuss that.

To my relief, Mary Beth buys my story that I felt sick to my stomach and was unable to make it to art this afternoon. "I just rested awhile in the library."

"You should've gone to the nurse," she says with concern. "Then she could've excused your absence."

"I was going to do that," I continue in my lie, "but I actually fell asleep in the lounge area."

She peers at me. "You don't look so good. Maybe you should go straight home. I can find a ride—"

"No, that's okay. I feel better now. I can drive you."

"After that, you better go straight home," she says as we walk to my car. "And take it easy. You don't want to be too sick to go to the dance—"

"The dance!" I let out a groan. "I forgot all about that."

"Wow, you really must be sick." She reaches over and touches my forehead. "Do you want me to drive?"

"No." I unlock the car. "I'll be fine."

"But what if it's the flu?" Mary Beth sounds really worried now. "What if you can't go to the dance tomorrow night?"

"I'll be okay. I think it was something I had for lunch."

"I hope so."

I let out a relieved sigh after Mary Beth gets out of the car. If anyone could figure me out and what I just did, it would be my best friend. Fortunately, she seems more concerned about my health than my conscience. As I drive toward my house, I tell myself that this was a one-time thing—a desperate measure, and my secret. A secret I shall take to the grave. I will never, *never* do it again. Then, determined to put it all behind me and wishing I could forget it, I go to bed.

· · · · · · · · · ·

I wake up to the sound of Mom quietly talking to me, putting a cool hand on my forehead . . . and for a moment I imagine I'm eight years old and getting over strep throat. "Are you okay?" Mom asks.

I open my eyes and look at her. She still has her hospital clothes on as well as a concerned look. "Yeah." I sit up and give a weak smile. "Just tired, I think." Rory hops down from the bed now, wagging his tail eagerly, as if he's had enough of this inactivity and is ready for some fun.

"Did you stay up late studying last night?" She cocks her head to one side. "I thought I noticed your light on when I got home."

I just nod.

She frowns. "You should know by now that cramming doesn't usually work. Slow and steady wins the race."

"I know."

She grips my chin, peering into my eyes, and turns my head from side to side as if she's examining me. I'm used to this — the life of a kid whose parents are doctors. "Well, you don't seem sick."

"I'm not." I push the covers off. "I feel just fine, Mom."

"But that nasty flu is running rampant." She goes over to turn on the overhead light. "And I told Dad that unless I was convinced you were perfectly fine, I was going to cancel tonight's plans."

"Tonight's plans?"

"The annual Christmas party at Dad's clinic. Remember? It's been on the calendar for a month now."

"Oh yeah." I stand and stretch. "The big bash."

She sighs. "Don't remind me. Anyway, I picked you up some Thai food for dinner — your favorite."

"Sounds great." I pull on my UGGs.

"I wish I could join you," Mom says as she pushes her bangs off her forehead. I notice that, like me, she has shadows beneath her eyes. "But as you can see, I'm in need of some intensive primping."

"Thanks for the takeout." I lean over to stroke Rory.

"And tomorrow evening, we'll be sure to stay home," she says from the doorway. "I told the hospital not to call me. I want to be around to enjoy your big night, GraceAnn."

"Oh, that's right." I remember now. "The dance."

"Do you think Uncle Russ will let you leave the pharmacy early? So you can get all dolled up and ready?"

"I'm sure five is early enough, Mom. It's not that big of a deal."

"Well, I think it's a big deal." She makes a sly smile. "And your dad's already digging out the video camera, planning to document the whole thing."

I groan dramatically. "Great. Can't wait."

. . . . . . . . . .

As I sit in the kitchen by myself, poking at lukewarm Pad Thai noodles, I realize that I'm not really hungry. In fact, my stomach feels like I swallowed a small bag of cement. I'm sure this is a side effect from what I did today. I still can't believe I really cheated. In fact, when I first woke from my nap, I thought perhaps it was all just a bad dream. Unfortunately, I know that's not the case. I did it . . . and there is no undoing it. My only consolation — and it's not much — is that I will never do it again. Never.

I feel a tiny bit better on Saturday. It helps going to work. I need the distraction, and I try to stay really busy, even doing the jobs no one likes to do, like thoroughly scrubbing down the bathrooms and "facing the shelves," which is the tedious process of dusting all the merchandise and moving it all forward so that the store portion of the pharmacy looks clean and freshly stocked . . . even though some of the merchandise is a little old.

"Are you feeling okay?" Aunt Lindsey asks me after lunch. She's manning the pharmacy today.

"Sure." I look up from where I'm stooped down rearranging the boxes of elastic bandages.

"You just seem awfully quiet."

I force a smile. "Just preoccupied."

"Your mom told me you're going to the Winter Ball." She looks on with interest. "Did you and Clayton get back together?"

I stand now. "No . . ." I say slowly. Then I explain about Bryant and Jorge. "I guess I'm feeling a little uncomfortable about it now." Okay, this is partially true, but it's not the real reason I'm being quiet. Still, it seems a good smoke screen. "And these guys aren't exactly youth group boys. Some people might even think that they're sort of, well, bad boys. But they're actually nice."

My aunt laughs. "GraceAnn with a bad boy? Now that's something I have a hard time imagining. Make sure your dad gets photos. I want to see this."

"I'll have him send them your way."

"Anyway, I wanted to ask if you'd make another delivery to Miss Julia this afternoon. I thought you could leave here around three and then just head on home."

"But that's two hours early."

"I know, but I won't clock you out until five. That will give you plenty of time to visit with Miss Julia and still get home with some extra time to spare for getting ready."

"All of it *on the clock*?" Uncle Russ can be a stickler about that sort of thing.

She grins. "Don't worry. I'm a co-owner here. I can change the rules if I want to sometimes. Just don't tell your uncle. Besides, Miss Julia is a valued customer and friend. And she specifically asked for you."

"Is she still feeling pretty bad?"

"I think she's improving. But it's hard on her being cooped up."

At three o'clock, I take the little bag of prescriptions and drive over to Miss Julia's house. This time she's dressed in pink velour warm-ups. But she still looks a little haggard and pale. "Come in, come in," she tells me as she opens the door wider. "Welcome to my humble hovel."

I hand her the bag. "How are you feeling?"

She makes a weary smile. "A little better."

"Oh, good. I'm sure it takes time to get well. But you do look better than the last time I saw you."

"Thank you." She pats her frazzled-looking white hair. "I missed my hairdresser appointment this week."

"Is there anything I can help you with?"

"Just come in and sit a spell." She leads the way into the living room. "Tell me about how you're doing, dear. Tell me what's going on in the outside world."

So I sit down and, for lack of anything else to say, tell her about the Winter Ball. And then to my surprise, I tell her about Clayton and how he broke my heart and how I hope my cranberry red dress will make him jealous. "I know that sounds silly and petty . . ."

She chuckles. "I think it sounds quite normal. In fact, I remember a time when I did something very similar to that."

She tells me a story about a boy she liked in college and how they were good friends and study partners. But to her dismay, he seemed more interested in her roommate than her. "And my roommate, her name was Lola, well, she was so glamorous and attractive. She looked a little like Bette Davis with her red lipstick and fancy clothes. And she smoked cigarettes too."

Miss Julia shook her head with disapproval. "So I tried to catch Howie's eye by imitating Lola." She laughed. "But smoking made me sick to my stomach, and I never looked very good in red lipstick either."

"But did you get his attention?"

"In a way, I did. Howie took me aside one day and told me I would do better to just be myself."

"That's nice. So did you start dating him then?"

She waved her hand. "Oh no, he married Lola that next summer."

"Oh . . ." I feel disappointed and sad for her.

"But really, I was thankful. Poor Howie turned into a horrible alcoholic and Lola was miserable. They both died young and unhappy." She stroked the cat in her lap and smiled. "I'm quite content with my little life, and oddly enough, it turned out just like Howie said to me years ago. It's better to just be myself."

I nod, taking this in.

"I'm sure you'd agree with me on that. You seem like the kind of girl who knows how to be herself."

I think back to the bracelet I snatched from Kelsey . . . and what I did . . . then look away.

"Oh, I'm sure there come times when you're not completely sure about who you are," she continues in a rambling sort of tone, "but that's just part of growing up. Eventually, you figure it out and the puzzle pieces fall into place. You realize being you is the best you can be."

"I hope so . . ."

"Just be true to yourself, GraceAnn." She points to the clock on the mantel. "Goodness, how time flies with you here, but I suspect you want to be on your way. I'm sure you'd rather be getting ready for your big night than sitting around here listening to old tales of days gone by."

"Don't be so sure of that," I say as I stand. "But my best friend, Mary Beth, would probably like it if I pick her up soon." I explain how we're going to get ready together and help each other with our hair.

"Yes, yes, be on your way, Cinderella." She chuckles. "And if you have any photos taken, perhaps you'll bring them by to share with me sometime. Or maybe I'll be able to get myself over to the pharmacy before long."

"You just take care and get well." I reach out to grasp her hand. "And thank you for sharing your stories with me."

As I drive to Mary Beth's, I consider Miss Julia's words about being true to myself. It's not like I haven't heard that kind of advice before. I mean, who hasn't? But for some reason it felt almost prophetic coming from her mouth. Like she had some idea of what I am dealing with. *I will never, never, never cheat again.* It is behind me now. I just wish I could forget about it.

## CHAPTER 6

"**Y**ou don't seem very excited," Mary Beth tells me as we make the final tweaks to our hair and makeup. "Are you feeling okay?"

I feign an enthusiastic smile. "Sure. I feel great."

"Tired from working all day?"

"Maybe." I sigh, trying to shove off this weight that seems to have attached itself to my spirits — the remnant guilt from yesterday. "But I'll be fine. I think I'm just hungry."

"That reminds me . . . Yesterday in art I overheard Jorge and Bryant, and it sounds like they're cooking up something special for dinner."

"They're cooking?" I stick in one last hairpin to secure my loose updo, frowning at how some of the hair is already slipping out.

"Well, I'm not sure they're actually cooking, but they seemed to be working on something." She looks concerned as she brushes on some blush. "But I have a feeling that neither of those guys has much money, so we better not set our expectations too high."

"As long as we get something to eat, I won't complain."

"And we definitely shouldn't expect a limo."

I just nod, then turn to look at her. "You look smashing, darling," I say with a fake British accent.

Mary Beth grins. "And you look stunning."

"Ready to face the cameras and crowds of adoring fans?" She giggles.

To our surprise, when we go out to where Mom and Dad are waiting, Mary Beth's mom is there as well. And a nice array of appetizers is set out on the island in the kitchen.

"Surprise," Mom says as Dad goes for his camera.

"You did this for us?" Mary Beth's eyes grow wide.

"Your mom and I did," my mom tells her. "For you and your dates."

"We thought it was one way to get them to linger a little," Mary Beth's mom says.

"So we can meet them." Dad snaps some candid shots. "Just to make sure they're respectable young men and not just trying to make off with our beautiful girls." He grins as he adjusts his camera lens.

"And you girls do look beautiful," Mom says as she adjusts a strap on my dress.

"So grown-up and sophisticated," Mary Beth's mom adds.

Before long, Rory is barking and the guys arrive. As Mary Beth and I meet them at the front door, I'm impressed by their interesting outfits. Jorge is wearing a mint green tuxedo that he says is from a thrift shop and straight out of the seventies. I can tell Mary Beth is impressed, and I'm starting to wonder if this random dance date thing might turn into something more with her. Her eyes light up even more as Jorge hands her a boxed wrist corsage of purple orchids.

"You look great," I tell Bryant as I admire his sleek-looking dark suit and narrow tie. "Where on earth did you get that suit?"

"It's from the sixties. It belonged to my grandfather." He smoothes his hand over his shaggy brown hair and nervously hands me a wrist corsage. It's similar to Mary Beth's, only my orchids are white. "My grandmother did some alterations to make it fit better."

I nod with approval. "It's perfect."

"You, uh, you look really nice too," he says politely.

"Thank you." I can tell he's really uneasy as he looks around — this must be way out of his comfort zone and I feel a little sorry for him — but at the same time, it's kind of cute too.

"I didn't know your parents were rich," he whispers to me.

I glance around the large foyer and shrug. "It's just a house."

"Our parents want to meet you," Mary Beth says. The guys exchange worried glances but follow as we lead them toward the kitchen, where introductions are made. And when the guys see the little feast laid out, they soon begin to relax. My dad gets more photos and takes some video, and finally it's time to leave.

But before we go, my dad stops the guys and gives them a very serious look. "Now, I realize how some kids think a dance like this is an excuse to drink alcohol and party, but I want to make it crystal clear to you boys that that is not only unaccept- able and illegal but I will personally come after both of you if I hear of anything like that happening tonight." His scowl melts into a charming smile, and I feel like crawling under a rock. *"Understand?"*

Bryant nods with a slightly shocked expression. "Yes, sir."

Mom laughs nervously. "You see, I work in the ER, and I see the results of that kind of thing far too much."

"No problem." Jorge holds up his hand like a pledge. "No alcohol. You've got our word."

"Good." Dad seems satisfied, and we say our good-byes and hurry out.

To my surprise, an old but gleaming, long silver car is parked in the driveway. "Whose is that?"

"That's my grandpa's too," Bryant admits. "It's not a limo, but I hope it'll do."

"It's great," I tell him. Okay, it looks a little like something out of a comic book, but it's also kind of interesting.

"It's better than great," Jorge says as the guys open the doors for us. "It's a 1964 Cadillac—and in mint condition. I can't believe your grandfather let you use it, man."

"First he made me wash and wax it and clean out the interior, then he made me swear on my grandmother's life that I would drive safely and return it looking as good as it looks now."

"This is so cool," Mary Beth says from the backseat. "I feel like we're starring in an old movie."

"This is fun." I nod. "Much better than a limo."

Bryant turns on the radio and a jazzy song comes on. "This is my grandfather's favorite station, but I can change it—"

"Don't you dare," Mary Beth says. "I love jazz."

"It's nice." Leaning back into the soft leather upholstery, I feel myself relaxing. And as I focus on the evening before us, the oppressive guilt that's been weighing on me might be lifting . . . slightly. Anyway, I am determined not to think about it tonight. Not after I see all the time and energy these guys are putting into our evening.

"So where are we eating?"

"It's a surprise," Bryant tells me as he drives toward town.

Then when we're in town, he drives slowly by some of the nicer restaurants, and I notice limos dropping off kids we know who, like us, are dressed to the nines. But Bryant continues past these places and on toward the less-impressive part of town, finally pulling into a dismal-looking strip mall. The car is quiet, and I'm sure Mary Beth is thinking what I'm thinking: Where are we going to eat here? I sure hope it's not Burger King. The only other eateries are a sandwich shop, which is closed, and a tiny taco shop called Rosita's, where a couple of other cars are parked.

"Here we are." Bryant parks right in front of Rosita's. "Jorge's choice for dinner."

"Oh . . . ?" Mary Beth gives me a concerned look as we get out.

I force a smile. "This should be interesting. Do they really have indoor seating in there? It looks tiny."

"Looks can be deceiving," Jorge says as he opens the front door. But once we're inside, this looks like a regular taco joint with a counter to order and menus printed on the wall behind it.

"Mr. Mendez," a plump Hispanic woman says to Jorge, "your table is waiting."

Jorge chuckles. "Thanks, Tia Rosita."

"Rosita is Jorge's aunt," Bryant tells me as the woman leads us past the few customers seated in the tiny dining area and opens a heavy door that goes into another small room. But this room looks totally different—it's like we just entered another world. A round table with a colorful striped tablecloth is attractively set with pottery dishes, silverware, pretty glasses, fresh flowers, and candles. And all around the edges of the tiled floor, luminaries light the room. And Mexican music plays pleasantly in the background.

"This is amazing," Mary Beth says as she walks around, admiring everything.

"It's beautiful, Jorge," I say.

"Jorge did it all himself," Rosita tells us proudly. "He is an artist."

"My mom helped," Jorge admits as we sit down. "These are her dishes."

The food turns out to be just as good as the setting, and the four of us have a truly enjoyable meal. By the time we're leaving to go to the dance, I think this date is incredibly pleasant. Would I have had any more fun if I'd gone to the ball with Clayton? Then I'm surprised that this is the first time I've thought of Clayton tonight. Am I over him?

For the first time since breaking up, I hope that I am over him. I really would like to be done with him. I almost don't care whether or not I make him jealous tonight. I glance over at Bryant and smile to see how handsome he looks in that suit, sitting behind the wheel of this big old Cadillac. This might end up being more than just a one-time thing for me too. Who knows?

When we get to the dance, the valet seems delighted to get the keys to the Cadillac, but Bryant warns him if there's so much as a scratch on it, his grandfather will hunt him down. Then he smiles . . . and I wonder if he's imitating my dad from earlier this evening. Was I wrong about the bad-boy image? I mean, Bryant can appear to be a bad boy, but judging by his actions, he's really quite nice. Just the same, I don't mind that people watching us might think otherwise. For some reason it feels fun and slightly risky to walk in with him.

"Right this way, ladies." Jorge holds out his arm for Mary Beth. Bryant does the same, and feeling festive and full of happy anticipation, I link my arm in his as we go into the hotel lobby, which is merrily decorated for Christmas. We're nearly to the ballroom where the dance is being held when Mary Beth mentions a need to use the ladies' room. As we both excuse ourselves, the guys promise to get us some punch.

"Isn't this turning out to be fun?" she says to me.

"I know. Who'd have thought?"

We both go into the stalls, and I hear others entering, chattering as they gather in front of the mirror. One of the girls sounds just like Kelsey Nelson, and suddenly I remember the last time Kelsey and I were in the restroom together—and how I confronted her and ripped off the cheater's bracelet. For that reason, I'm not exactly eager to exit the stall. So I linger.

"Oh, Sean's car is nothing," Kelsey is saying to the other girl. "I mean, it's nice enough, but you should see the Mustang my stepdad has promised to get me."

"Yeah, sure," the other girl says sarcastically, "but that's only if you get an A in AP Biology. How likely is that?"

"You'd be surprised," Kelsey says lightly. "I'm a lot more academic than you realize."

The other girl laughs and then they both leave. I just stand there in the stall—speechless—trying to comprehend what I just heard, lining it up against what Kelsey said to me just yesterday.

"GraceAnn?" Mary Beth calls out. "Are you okay?"

I flush the toilet, adjust my dress, and step out.

"Are you feeling sick or something?" She peers curiously at me.

"No . . . not exactly." I frown as I wash my hands.

"You sure? Because you look pale." She glances at me as she freshens her lip gloss.

"Was that Kelsey Nelson I heard talking just now?" I slowly dry my hands.

"Yeah. She was bragging to Destiny about how her stepdad is going to get her a car. A Mustang I think she said." Mary Beth laughs and hands me her lip gloss. "That is if she gets an A in AP Biology."

I frown as I put on some lip gloss.

"Oh, that's right. She's the cheater, isn't she?" Mary Beth shakes her head as I hand her back her lip gloss. "Sad, isn't it?"

I just nod, feeling sick inside again. What I thought was turning into a perfect evening feels ruined. Soiled. And it's all my fault.

But as we walk back to the ballroom, I start to feel angry at Kelsey. I think of how she lied to me, how she played the pitiful victim . . . acting like her horrible stepdad was going to beat her senseless unless she passed AP Biology. For a "smart" girl, I am very stupid. And naive.

I'd like to storm over to Kelsey, who is now standing near the center of the room, surrounded by her insulation of friends. Just the same, I'd like to break into that group, interrupt their chitchat and gossip, and loudly tell Kelsey that I overheard her in the bathroom—and that I'm enraged. I'd like to confront her for lying to me about her stepdad, and let her know that as a result of her dishonesty, my promise "not to tell" is now permanently revoked, and that first thing Monday morning, I'll be going to the dean to report what I saw, complete with my evidence, and that she will most definitely be suspended, not only from classes but her beloved cheerleading as well.

Except I can't do that now.

As much as it sickens me to be aligned with someone like Kelsey Nelson, it's too late. I compromised myself by following her stupid, stupid, stupid example. And now all I can do is stand by and watch the aftermath.

How is it that she seems to feel no guilt or remorse whatsoever? Meanwhile I am drowning in it. It all seems so unfair. So unjust.

"Something wrong?" Bryant asks me as he hands me a cup of red punch.

I force a smile. "No, I was just thinking."

He grins. "I like that you're a thinking kind of girl."

The knot in my stomach grows tighter as I nod. How I wish that were still true. As we dance, I try not to think about how Bryant's opinion of me would change if he knew who I really was . . . what I'd done . . . only yesterday.

I see Clayton dancing with Avery. He's dressed in a handsome tux but not looking nearly as interesting as Bryant. Even Avery's cream-colored dress seems a little drab and predictable. For Clayton's sake, I try to act much happier than I'm feeling right now. And I can tell it bothers him. A while later, I even catch him gazing at me, almost longingly or perhaps with regret. It's everything I had hoped for tonight. And yet I get no satisfaction.

As the evening progresses, I feel myself becoming more and more obsessed with Kelsey Nelson. I can't seem to escape the painful realization of how she's such a lying cheat. Or how she pulled me into her selfish schemes. Or how she so cleverly tricked me into feeling sorry for her. It keeps running through my mind like the headline on a reader board: Airheaded Cheerleader Triumphs Over Academic Nerd.

Oh sure, I know I had a choice in the matter. I could've done it all differently. But like a dope, I fell for the bait. I almost wonder if she didn't plan it all like that. Perhaps she wanted me to keep her bracelet and use it the way I did. That way I'd be in just as deep as she is.

As I dance and smile and laugh, putting on the act of my life, all in the hopes that Bryant isn't too disappointed in his date—especially after the time and effort he's invested in tonight—all I can think of is that I am a complete and utter fool. As we dance to the music, four words keep reverberating through my brain, repeating themselves with the beat: *You're such a fool, you're such a fool, you're such a fool . . .*

On Sunday morning, my dad comes into my room with a big grin. "We have a surprise for you today. Get up and get dressed ASAP."

"Are we going to church?" I look groggily at my clock to see it's barely eight. I didn't get home until after one last night, and then I didn't sleep well.

"No, we'll miss church today. But it'll be worth it. You'll see."

So not knowing what I'm in for, I get dressed and let Rory out into the backyard, then go out to find my parents already in the car. "Let's get out of here," Dad says, backing his car out of the garage. "We'll nab a bite to eat on our way."

"And the sooner we're out of town, the better," Mom explains. "Just in case the hospital calls and tries to get me to come in to work."

Before long, Dad's on the freeway, and after about an hour, he finally stops at a Starbucks and we get coffee and pastries to go. "Just enough to tide us over until we get there," he tells me. "We have reservations for lunch."

We're going north, but I have no idea what the destination is . . . nor do I care. After I finish my coffee and muffin, I fall asleep. When I wake up, the car has stopped and Dad is getting out.

"Here we are," he announces as he opens the back door.

I sit up and blink, getting my bearings. *"Where?"*

"Stanford." Mom hands me an envelope. "It came in yesterday's mail, and with all the excitement over the dance, I forgot to tell you about it."

"It's opened," I say as I slip out the crisp letter and examine the impressive Stanford heading on the stationery.

"Sorry," she says. "But I was dying of curiosity, and Dad said it was okay so I took a peek. Congratulations, GraceAnn!"

I'm skimming the words, but it's clearly an acceptance letter. "I'm accepted," I say quietly. "I'm really accepted."

"Congratulations!" Dad grins and reaches for my hand. "Now, come on, sleepyhead, we're burning daylight."

I grab my bag and allow my dad to pull me from the car. *"Stanford?"* I look around, taking in yellow adobe buildings, red tile roofs, palm trees. It's very pretty, but I can't quite believe it. All this feels like a fantasy . . . maybe I'm still sleeping. "Is this for real?"

"We're going to check out the campus and have some lunch," Mom explains. "It seemed the perfect way to celebrate. Are you surprised?"

"I'm totally shocked." I've been dreaming of coming up here to visit for a couple of years now, and my parents have promised . . . but it just never worked out. Until today.

"You've been working so hard in school." Mom takes my hand as we walk. "And we're so proud of your accomplishments. And then to find out about your acceptance. Well, we decided it was time to get you up here."

"A friend told me about a good restaurant on campus," Dad

says. "We have reservations at one. We will celebrate royally."

"I printed out a map of the campus." Mom digs in her bag and starts pointing things out to me.

We walk around for about an hour, and I come out of my daze and eventually discover that Stanford is even better in real life than it was in dreams or the photos on the website. It's like love at first sight with this campus. I feel right at home here. I won't admit it to my parents, but it was nothing like this when they took me to an alma-mater event at the University of Southern California a few years ago.

But I know they want me to go to Stanford as much as I do. They've both said, on numerous occasions, how they'd wanted to come here themselves, but grades and finances kept them from coming. Somehow they both ended up at USC, which is where they met and fell in love, so I guess it wasn't such a bad deal after all. But now that I've got the acceptance letter tucked safely in my purse, they seem certain that nothing will keep me from coming here. To them, it's in the bag.

And maybe it is. My temporary slump in grades is just that—*temporary*. I am determined to do better from this day forward. And even my slipup on Friday can't keep me from coming here. At least I don't think it can. I just need to buckle down and focus—starting tomorrow. And to my great relief, I no longer feel miserable about my breakup with Clayton. That, too, is behind me. I can't believe I let it get to me like I did. What was wrong with me?

By the time we're eating lunch, I feel positive and enthusiastic. Okay, there's still a trace of guilt and regret coursing beneath the surface. Like each time my parents mention how great I'm doing in school, how impressive my class loads have been, how outstanding my grades are, how proud they are of me . . . stuff like that feels like a dagger to my gut. But I try not to show it.

"You probably have an excellent chance of being class valedictorian," Dad tells me. "You know your mother was valedictorian." He pats Mom's hand.

"Yes, in a tiny school," she says. "Being first in a class of 107 students isn't as impressive as GraceAnn's class. Aren't there about 500 kids in your class?"

"Yes, and I seriously doubt I'll be valedictorian," I tell them. And considering how fall term has gone, I'd say this is a pretty sure bet. In fact, I can name at least three other students who have a GPA equal to mine . . . maybe higher by the time this term's grades are made public.

"And that's just fine," Mom assures me. "We're still very proud of you."

"And Harvard still isn't out of the picture," Dad says. "Earl's son didn't get his acceptance until early spring."

After lunch we walk around campus some more, and by the time we leave, I feel truly hopeful. I can imagine myself attending classes here. Less than a year from now. And it's exciting.

On the way home, I text message Mary Beth, telling her where I'm at and about my acceptance letter and how it's been an awesome day. Then seeing a message from Bryant, I text him as well, thanking him again for a great night, and then I tell him where I'm at and about getting accepted. Okay, I suppose I'm a little bit proud. Who wouldn't be?

· · · · · · · · · ·

Later that evening as I'm studying for my upcoming finals, Bryant calls me. "Congratulations on being accepted at Stanford."

"Thanks!" I close my laptop and lean back on my bed. It's about time for a little break.

"I haven't heard anything back from the schools I've applied to."

For some reason I'm surprised he's applying at all. I still have this bad-boy image of Bryant. An image I need to shake. "What schools have you applied to?"

He lists some off, then admits that UCLA is his first choice and how he wants to pursue something in the arts or film.

"That sounds like fun," I say.

"And what will you major in, or do you know yet?"

"Probably some form of medicine . . . like my parents."

"That sounds serious, but interesting."

"I guess." I don't admit that it just sounds normal to me. When you grow up with doctors for parents, medicine can seem almost boring.

"You're such a brainiac. I'm sure you'd make a great doctor." He chuckles. "I know I'd come to you if I was sick."

"And maybe when I'm a famously rich doctor, I'll commission some art from you."

"Or come watch my movies in the theater," he adds.

"Absolutely."

"Your goals are probably more realistic than mine," he says a bit sadly.

"I don't see why."

"Because you're already off to such a great start, GraceAnn. You've taken school seriously. All those AP classes and trigonometry. Just like Jorge. Now that I'm a senior, I'm wishing I'd done it differently. I think of all the time I wasted just being a goof-off, and now I'm getting worried that I might end up paying for it later. In the meantime, you've been doing everything right. And I guess, well, I can't help but admire that."

I don't say anything. Instead of receiving what I know he means as a compliment, I feel guilty again. If only he knew the truth.

"But maybe I'll be inspired by you," he says cheerfully. "Maybe I'll take more challenging classes for the rest of the year. You think I could get into some of your AP classes?"

"I don't see why not. I'm sure you're every bit as smart as I am, Bryant. It's just that you haven't applied yourself."

He laughs. "You sound like my dad."

"But that doesn't mean it's too late."

"I hope not. Okay, I've made up my mind. You're going to be my inspiration, GraceAnn, and by the time I graduate, I want to be known around school as an academic geek too."

"Does that mean you're going to get rid of that cool motor-cycle jacket?"

"Hmm . . . you like that?"

"Of course. Maybe you can become an academic but just leave off the geek part."

"Sounds good to me."

"The more I get to know you, the more I wonder about your tough-guy/bad-boy image."

"What do you mean?"

"You're not really like that, Bryant. Underneath."

He chuckles. "You mean you thought I looked like a tough guy?"

"I guess. Although I should know better than to judge a book by its cover."

"What about your image?" he asks.

"What image?"

"Miss Perfect."

I let out a groan. "I hate that image."

"Really?"

"Okay, sometimes I hate it. Sometimes I probably do everything I can to perpetuate it. I don't even understand it myself."

"Do you think we create exterior images to protect what's underneath?"

I'm slightly taken aback by the depth of this statement. "Uh . . . yeah."

"I mean, it's kind of an old cliché," he continues. "Acting tough to hide a tender heart. Trying to act perfect to hide the imperfections beneath."

Now this makes me really uncomfortable because I know I am very far from perfect and I don't want anyone — not even Bryant — to know about the very real imperfections. So I change the subject. "I'm curious; what's the story behind your tattoo?"

He laughs.

"Come on, please tell me."

"Maybe someday, Lowery."

I cringe to hear him calling me by my last name again.

"Sorry, I mean *GraceAnn*. And maybe I'll tell you about it someday. After we've gotten to know each other better."

But I get it. He is gently reminding me that there are reasons to keep up our exterior images — until we trust each other more. And really, I'm not ready to open up too much either. Even so, we talk another hour or so until his phone battery gets so low that we end the conversation.

After I close my phone, I realize I like this guy more and more. And I'm thinking of Clayton less and less. I also realize that it's past eleven and I didn't finish the studying I'd planned to do, but if I don't turn out my light, my parents will be checking on me.

As I get into bed, snuggling up against Rory's warm furry back, I comfort myself with the knowledge that finals don't actually start until Tuesday. And that buys me a little more time.

· · · · · · · · · ·

By Monday morning, I feel charged and energized and ready to face the week before me. I know I've made some mistakes, but I believe those are surmountable now. I will move forward and put them behind me. Onward and upward.

"You seem a lot happier today," Mary Beth says as we're on our way to school.

"I am. I feel hopeful."

"Because of the Stanford letter?"

"Partly. But it's more than that. For starters, the Winter Ball turned out to be so much better than expected."

"For sure." She lets out a happy sigh. "Jorge came over yesterday."

"To your house?"

"Yeah. Mom even invited him to stay for dinner, and he did."

"You never told me that."

She shrugs. "I really like him, GraceAnn."

"That's cool."

"Who would've thunk?"

I giggle. "Yeah, who would've?"

"What about you and Bryant?"

"Bryant's cool. And I can tell that we're off to a good friendship."

"But nothing more than that?"

"I don't know . . ." I frown at the red light. "Considering

how devastated I was after Clayton dumped me, I suppose I'm a little gun-shy, you know?"

"That's probably wise. You don't want to have a rebound romance with Bryant."

"That's true. For now we'll just be friends." I chuckle. "Good friends, I hope."

"I noticed Clayton ogling you at the Winter Ball."

I roll my eyes.

"You must've seen him too."

"Maybe . . . I mean, sure, I saw him." I don't admit to her that I also saw him kissing Avery in the hallway. As much as I wish it didn't, that hurt a lot. But I just can't bring myself to say it now. Mostly I want to think I'm moving on. "I know it might be hard to believe, but I don't really care about him anymore. I'm not going to think about him." I let out a big sigh, hoping that this is true.

"That's probably why you feel better today."

"Maybe. But I also had a pretty great weekend." Now I tell her more about visiting Stanford and how at home I felt there. "It was like déjà vu or something, like I'd been there before or maybe just that I belong there. It was so cool."

"I can't believe we won't be in school together next year," she says sadly. "I'm going to miss you so much."

"I wish you could go to Stanford too. You'd love it there, Mary Beth. It's really pretty, and it has an artsy feel you'd appreciate."

"Even if we could afford it — and we can't — I'd never get accepted." She looks slightly depressed now and that makes me feel bad.

"Who knows . . . maybe they won't want me either." I turn into the school parking lot. "Maybe I'll end up at the same college as you."

"You bet, GraceAnn, I'm sure that'll happen."

"You never know." I reach for my bag. "My grades this term are still a little shaky. Things could change."

"Not for you," she tells me as we walk toward the front entrance. "You're kind of like a golden girl—good things just keep coming your way."

I can't help but laugh at that. However, I wish it was true. I wish good things would keep coming my way. And maybe if I work harder, they will.

## CHAPTER 8

There's a spring in my step as I go to my first class. I'm early enough to be the first one to go through the test file. Mr. VanDorssen alphabetically files students' tests in a crate, and it's up to us to collect them. He says it's a form of time and energy conservation—his.

I find my paper and pull it out, but what I see on the top, written in blood-red ink, sends an electric jolt from the top of my head to the tips of my toes: F. I got an F. A big stinkin' F.

Other students are coming in, and I hold the paper against my chest so no one else can see my grade and hurry to get a desk in the back of the room. I don't usually sit in the back of any classroom, but today it's the only place I care to be. If I could do it without penalty, I'd probably skulk out of here and go sit in my car until second period . . . or all day.

As students pick up their tests and find their seats, I sneak furtive peeks at my paper. Then after everyone is seated and class has begun, I go over my test more carefully, trying to figure out where I blew it, where I used a wrong formula or mistyped on my calculator, but I'm so upset that I can't even think clearly or scientifically anymore. It's like my brain went into a shutdown mode.

I take some deep breaths and attempt to calm myself. Then going more slowly, I look over the pages again. This time I resort to third-grade math to figure out what percentage of the problems I missed. I feel slightly relieved that I got more than half correct. At least I'm not a total loser. Well, except for that big red F at the top of the page.

When class is done, I remain in my seat as the others exit, then I hurry to the front and hold up my paper. "I know I've fallen behind," I tell him. "But I'm shocked that I got an F."

Mr. VanDorssen gives me a blank look.

"I mean, I can see that the problems I missed were clearly mistakes. But I just don't understand how getting half of the answers correct would result in an F. It doesn't seem fair."

"GraceAnn, you're smart enough to know that I grade on the bell curve. Do you want me to make a drawing for you?" He nods to the chalkboard behind him. "I could demonstrate how it works if you like."

"I know how it works."

He nods and removes his glasses. "I thought you did. The problem is that you've fallen behind. I'm not sure why." He frowns. "You had a solid B average before, didn't you?"

I feel another small jolt of shock because I actually thought it was better than that, but I don't say this.

He rubs the bridge of his nose. "So if you get a good mark on your final tomorrow, you might be able to pull your grade up to . . . well, probably a C at best."

"A C at best?" I stare at him in horror.

"No guarantees."

"But I just got accepted into Stanford."

He smiles. "Congratulations."

I hold up the paper. "But a C? At best? Can't you see how

that's going to pull down my GPA?"

He shrugs. "It is what it is."

Now the students for second period are coming in.

"Study hard," he tells me as I'm leaving.

I want to shout something terrible back at him. Fortunately I have the sense and self-control not to. But as I hurry out, I know I have to do something. For starters, I will not be taking trig next term. No way. What I'll do about this F and tomorrow's test is a mystery. But I'm an intelligent person; there must be a way to figure this out.

I'm still obsessing over it by lunchtime. Even with Bryant and Jorge joining Mary Beth and me at our regular table, I find it hard to interact and converse.

"What's eating her?" Jorge asks Mary Beth.

"Bad grade," she says quietly.

"Tell the world," I say hotly to her.

"Sorry." She looks hurt. "I didn't know it was a secret."

I roll my eyes, then shake my head. "Sorry. It's not a secret. But it's not like I want to go shouting it from the rooftops either." The truth is, Mary Beth doesn't even know how bad the grade really is. I simply told her I was disappointed. If she knew I got an F, she'd probably be nearly as worried as I am.

"Sorry about that," Bryant tells me in a sympathetic way. "Which class was it in?"

"Trig," I mutter as I fork into my salad.

"Well, at least it wasn't the grade for your final," he points out. "Maybe you'll do better on that."

I give him a hopeless look. "Maybe . . ."

As they start talking about a singer on YouTube, arguing about whether he's really any good or not, I stand up and gather my stuff. It's a lot earlier than necessary, even for someone as late-phobic as I am, but I just want to escape.

"I need to get something from the library," I tell them as I pick up my tray. I doubt they believe me, but I don't really care. Mostly I just want to be alone for a few minutes. I want to clear my head and come up with some kind of escape plan. But because my next class is AP Biology, I slowly head toward the math and science department. Thinking and walking, and walking and thinking.

As I round a corner, I notice what looks like Kelsey Nelson's back. Her boyfriend, a jock named Drew, has his arms wrapped around her and they're in the midst of a long, passionate kiss (which is actually against school rules), so fortunately they're oblivious to me.

Still, I'm embarrassed to catch them like this and don't want to walk past them, so I duck into the nearby restroom and give them a minute to finish up their silly interlude. Maybe a teacher will happen by and give them a citation. That would be nice.

Just as I'm about to leave, Kelsey comes in. *"Oh!"* She jumps as if frightened. "What are you, some kind of bathroom freak?"

"Is there a law against using the restroom now?" I imitate her surly tone as all my anger toward her bubbles to the surface. "Kind of like cheating or making out in the hallway."

"Sorry, GraceAnn." With a sugary smile, she turns to the mirror and starts to fix her smeared makeup. "You just caught me by surprise, that's all. How are you doing?"

I go and stand next to her, locking gazes with her big blues in the dimly lit mirror. "As a matter of fact, I'm not doing too well. But you must be feeling pretty great these days. I hear your stepdad is rewarding you with a Mustang for acing AP Biology this term."

Her eyes get bigger. "Who told you that?"

"You did." I narrow my eyes. "I overheard you in the restroom at the dance."

"You really are a bathroom lurker."

"So are you," I point out. "Anyway, I heard the whole thing."

She frowns. "That really should teach me not to drink and talk." She laughs like this is clever.

"You lied to me," I continue in a seething tone. "You gave me your poor-little-me sob story, and it was all a great big lie."

"I'm sorry." She turns to face me. "But you had me so shook up. It was just the first thing that came into my head. Really, GraceAnn, I'm sorry."

"I should've told on you."

"But you didn't." She places a hand on my shoulder. "Because you really are a good person."

I want to scream at her. Why does everyone keep acting like I'm so good?

"And what I told you about my life being over if I got kicked off the cheerleading squad is absolutely true. I would be totally devastated. You have to know *that's* not a lie. I swear I would want to kill myself."

"Stop being so melodramatic."

"Are you going to tell?" She's truly frightened now.

I shrug, enjoying this little cat-and-mouse game, watching her squirm.

"Is there something I can do to make it up to you?" she pleads. *"Anything?"*

I roll my eyes.

"Do you still have the, uh, the evidence?" she asks quietly.

The truth is, I flushed it down the toilet. But I don't think she needs to know this. For some reason, probably because misery loves company, I want to make her suffer a bit more.

"Really, GraceAnn, I'm truly sorry for lying to you about my stepdad. I shouldn't have done that. And if there's anything I can do to make it up to you, please tell me."

The first bell rings, and I realize that this silly game I'm playing is just a waste of my time and breath. "Forget about it," I mutter as I turn to leave. But as I go to class, I feel a smidgeon of satisfaction for scaring her like that. It wasn't much, but it was worth something.

As a student hands out last week's exams, my previous bad spirits are replaced with an unexpected rush of pleasure when I see the A plus at the top of my test paper. I blink and stare hard . . . then remember — of course, I cheated.

Feeling like I need to hide it, like it's a pair of dirty underwear that fell out of my purse, I slip the test inside my notebook and attempt to focus as Ms. Bannister goes over a litany of information she thinks we should have memorized by now and what might be part of Thursday's final exam.

I listen and take copious notes, but I'm distracted. One thought keeps repeating itself through my mind. The reason I got such a low grade in trig was because almost everyone else in the class was cheating. How people cheat in trig is not absolutely clear to me, but I just know — deep down in my gut — that cheating has to be going on. It's the only explanation for what's messing up that stupid bell curve.

And so I begin to reason: If cheating is the way students secure good grades, perhaps that's supposed to be part of our education. We're expected to learn how to cheat and how to do it well enough to: (1) not get caught and (2) secure a good grade despite the stupid bell curve. Maybe it's just part of the education game.

And maybe I'm going to the dark side or maybe I'm temporarily insane, but my mind begins to devise a plan, and as soon as the release bell rings, I get Kelsey's attention on our way out the door. "I want to talk to you." I guide her out into the hallway and over to a quiet alcove.

"What is it now?" She looks worried again. But I can tell I still have a hold over her. She can't just blow me off.

"You said you'd do anything to make up for lying to me, right? So I won't tell on you."

She nods nervously. "What do you want? Money?"

I laugh. "Hardly."

"What then?"

"Tell me your source."

"My source?"

"Who gives you the answers? Who do you connect with?"

Her brows arch high. "You're kidding."

I shake my head. "I'm not."

"I can't tell you."

"Tell me or I'm going to the dean right this minute."

She looks truly frightened now. "Why do you want to know?"

I think hard. "Maybe I hope I can do something about it."

"Do something? Like what?"

"Like warn this person that he or she better stop doing this before they get into serious trouble."

She looks slightly amused, like she knows this is not going to happen.

"Who is it, Kelsey?"

"Really, I can't tell you."

"Tell me, or you're going down." I give her my best threatening look. "I mean it."

"He'll kill me, GraceAnn."

"He doesn't have to know who told me. I'll keep you out of it. You just get me connected to him. *Okay?*" I'm making this up as I go. "I just want to have a conversation with him, to try to talk some sense into him about all this. Really, he needs to stop. It's wrong."

"Maybe so . . . but I don't know . . . he might come after me."

I shrug. "Fine. Then I'm going to the dean right now." I start to walk away.

"No." She firmly grips my arm. "I'll tell you."

And just like that, with kids walking and talking just a few feet from us, Kelsey tells me her source: Dirk Zimmerman. I remember Dirk. He graduated from here last year. Some kids called him Dirtbag Dirk. Only behind his back, of course. Now Kelsey pulls up his number on her phone, shows it to me, and I enter it into mine. "Just please keep me out of this," she begs.

"I only want to talk to him," I assure her. And then we go our separate ways. Feeling like a secret agent, I hurry outside. I know I shouldn't be doing this — on so many levels — but I pull out my cell phone and dial his number. Part of me is hoping he won't answer or it will be disconnected or anything to end what could turn into an ugly train wreck. But a guy answers, and I just go ahead and jump in.

"I heard that you can help me with some test answers," I quietly tell him.

"Who are you, and how did you get my number?"

"My name's GraceAnn Lowery," I say unsteadily.

"Not the academic girl from Magnolia Park High?"

I can't believe he remembers me. "Yes, that's me."

He laughs. "So tell me, why are you calling me?"

"Because I need your help."

"How did you get my name?"

"A friend . . . one of your clients."

"Who?"

"I promised not to say. But she assured me you would help me."

"I *might* help you. But let me warn you: If this is a sting, you're in way over your head. It's been tried before and it never works. It always ends badly for someone. Just not me." He laughs.

"I swear it's not a sting." And just like that I'm telling him how I fell behind and how I need to maintain my average in order to enroll at Stanford next year.

"Yeah, I get a lot of business from you academic geeks. You act like you're so smart in school, but the truth is, you're probably dumber than the rest of us."

"So, will you help me?"

He tells me to meet him at the 7-Eleven on El Dorado Drive at 4:00 p.m. sharp, then he hangs up. I hurry to my next class, knowing that I'm at least five minutes late.

I don't have to do this. I shouldn't do this. I won't do this.

But by 3:48 p.m., after acting perfectly normal as I dropped Mary Beth at her house, I am pulling into the 7-Eleven parking lot. My heart feels like it might jump right out of my chest, and my stomach feels like it's twisted upside down and sideways. I know, without a doubt, this is wrong. *Wrong, wrong, wrong.* But it's like I have no choice. Like my back is against the bell curve wall, and this is the only way out.

I park my car on the backside of the convenience store. Far enough from the front door to go unnoticed, but near enough to watch the parking lot. I want to keep a low profile . . . just in case someone I know comes in here. For some reason I feel like it's obvious that I am up to no good. Like it's written all over my face: *This girl is a liar and a cheater.*

I check my watch, counting the seconds and minutes ticking by. It's not too late to run. I can still back out. Dirk might know my name and phone number, but it's not like he'd come looking for me. At least I don't think so.

At 4:04 p.m., just as I'm ready to give up on what I know is a bad idea, I see a late-model black SUV pulling into the parking lot. The windows are tinted black so I can't see who's inside, but I have a feeling it's him.

To get a better look, I get out of my car and act like I'm going into the store. Maybe I'll even buy a soda. But as I put my hand on the door, I hear someone calling my name. I turn to see the passenger-side window open slightly, and Dirk tells me to get inside.

Suddenly I'm not sure about this. I was taught as a child never to get into a car with strangers. But I was also told not to lie, cheat, or steal. Shoving down the little voice inside me that's saying "no, no, no!" I open the door and slide into the passenger seat.

"Hey, Dirk." I nervously glance around at the slick interior, noticing that this ride comes with all the bells and whistles. "Is this how you usually do business?"

He shrugs, studying me closely. "Depends."

"Well, I've never done this before . . . and maybe it's not such a good idea." I move my hand to the door handle, ready to bolt if he tries to take off with me still in here. "In fact, I think I've changed my mind, Dirk. Sorry to bother you like—"

"Wait a minute. Are you chickening out?"

I give him a sheepish smile. "Maybe."

"So you're willing to flunk out of some classes because you're afraid?"

"Well, I . . ."

"Look, kid, it's up to you. Go ahead and run if you want. It's not my problem if you want bad grades. I got better things to do. But like I warned, don't turn vigilante and think you're going to turn me in. I could ruin you like that." He snaps his fingers.

The image of Stanford's campus flashes through my mind, the proud expectant looks on my parents' faces as we celebrated my acceptance letter. "No," I say slowly. "I'm not leaving. I need your help." Then I tell him the two classes I need answers for.

"No problem. I have computer programs for all the trig tests, and the AP Biology final is simple."

Just like that? He makes it sound so easy. I stare at him for a moment. He's a little on the pudgy side, and his eyes seem small and beady on his broad, ruddy face. If I saw him on the street, I wouldn't give him a second look, and there's nothing about his appearance that would suggest he's running an academic cheating business. Yet it seems obvious that's what he does. I know this SUV doesn't come cheap. And I can't imagine why Kelsey would send me down the wrong path since I have the power to take her down.

Still I wonder, *How can I trust this creep?* More than that I wonder, *How did I get to this place?*

## CHAPTER 9

"Here's the deal," Dirk tells me. "It's $250 for each exam. So that's $500. And for obvious reasons, I only deal in cash."

"*Five hundred dollars!*"

"Is that a problem for you?"

"I don't know . . . I just didn't expect it to be so much."

"What's it worth to you to go to Stanford?"

He has a point. Even so . . . "That's a lot of money."

"Take it or leave it." He tips his head to the door. "I got better things to do than sit here and squabble over it with you."

I sigh loudly. It feels like I'm climbing deeper and deeper into a black hole, like I'll never be able to climb out again.

"You don't have the money?" He sounds irritated now. "Why did you call me and ask me to help you if you don't have the money?"

"I *have* the money. I was just calculating how many hours I'll have to work to make that much."

"Where do you work at?"

"Lowery's Drugstore," I absently say as I finish the math, realizing that it will take me almost seven Saturdays to make that up in my back account. That won't be until February.

"Okay, kid, maybe I can cut you a special deal."

I turn to him hopefully. "A special deal?"

"Since this is your first time doing business with me. I do that sometimes . . . if I feel like it."

"That'd be great," I say weakly. "What kind of deal?"

"Half price."

"So only $250 for *both* exams?"

"Sure. But it's a one-time-only thing. And don't go shooting your mouth off about it to anyone. Understand?"

"Believe me, I don't want *anyone* to know I'm doing this."

"Yeah, you academic geeks have to maintain your perfect little images." He chuckles in an evil, twisted way.

I'm tempted to lay into him now, to point out that it's jerks like him who make people like me (normally honest and law-abiding) do things like this. I want to scream at him — demanding to know why he thinks it's okay to mess up the system, ruin the bell curve, and take advantage of students like me . . . except that I don't want to ruin my chances of rescuing my GPA. And, after all, he is giving me a good deal. Why rock the boat? I know I'm a wimp . . . a lying, cheating, pathetic wimp.

"So if I cut this deal for you, you better be good to me in return. For starters, that means you can send trusted referrals my way. That's how my business grows."

I bite my lip. "Well, I don't know if I can do that."

He frowns. "Then just remember, GraceAnn, you owe me one. I don't give everyone this good of a deal."

I nod. "And I appreciate it." Okay, now I'm wondering what he means by that? What kind of repayment does he expect? Or is he just jerking me around . . . because he can?

"So you have the cash then?"

"Not on me. But I can get it."

"When do you need the answers by?"

"I need the trig ones for tomorrow."

"No problemo."

"And I need the AP Biology answers for Thursday."

"You got 'em. As soon as I get the money, you get the goods. No money, no answers. That's how I work."

"How do you get them to me?" I hope he doesn't plan to come to my house to deliver them.

"It's all done through e-mail. The program for trig is easy to load into your calculator. I send you the instructions and everything you need."

"Where do you get this stuff anyway?" I know he can't be smart enough to make it himself.

He narrows his beady eyes. "No questions."

"Okay."

"So where do you want me to pick up the cash? Your house? The bank? What?"

I look at my watch and see it's nearly four thirty. "I have enough time to make it to the bank. I guess you can meet me there." Then I tell him which branch, and with shaky knees, I get back into my car. Suddenly it's like I'm on autopilot, like I've done this before or am programmed to do it now. I drive to the bank, go inside, make a withdrawal from my savings, smile at the teller as I thank her, walk outside, and there, parked next to the driver's side of my car, is the black SUV. It looks like a Mafia car.

"Get in," he tells me through the partially opened window.

I glance around but don't see anyone watching, so I hop in. "These tinted windows come in handy," I say as I reach into my bag for the cash. Am I really doing this? Is this really me?

He counts out the bills, then slips them into his inside jacket pocket. "Okay, this is how it goes down." He hands me a notepad. "Write your e-mail address here, unless you want to get a new account."

"A new account?"

"Some people create a new e-mail account so they can use it and lose it. You know, dump the whole thing later and bury the trail. That's up to you."

I think about this. "How would I get the new address to you? I mean, in time to get the stuff before my test tomorrow?"

"Good point. Better just use the one you have."

As I write down my e-mail address, he continues to explain. "Anyway, I have a bunch of different e-mail accounts, so I never tell anyone which one I'm using. And for some reason my e-mails sometimes end up as spam. So if it's not in your regular e-mail, make sure you go to your junk mail and look for the subject line 'Better Yourself.'"

"Better yourself?" I repeat this, trying not to consider the irony.

"Yeah. The answers and the instructions of how to load and use the trig stuff are in the attachments. And don't worry, I have the latest virus protection on my computer so my docs are always safe to open."

Again the irony hits me. *Safe* to open . . . *better* yourself . . . it's almost laughable. Except that I feel like crying.

"Okay, that's it." Dirk sticks out his hand to shake hands with me. I feel like a fool . . . like I'm sealing this shady deal . . . like I just sold my soul to the devil. "And don't worry. None of my clients ever get caught. Not from my end anyway. If you blow it, then it's your fault. But the smart kids figure it out."

"Right . . ." I feel sick, almost like I'm going to vomit.

He smiles. "And don't feel guilty. You'd be shocked to know how many kids are doing this. It's like an epidemic."

I just nod and reach for the door handle. "Thanks," I mumble.

"Good luck, kid!"

I take in a deep breath as I unlock my car. Then as his SUV rumbles away, I get inside and just sit there. What have I done? *What have I done?*

As I drive home, I'm in a daze, trying to wrap my head around all that just transpired. By the time I go into the house, where I'm relieved to see no one's home, I convince myself that I just kissed $250 good-bye. I know Dirk has pulled a fast one on me. Maybe Kelsey is in on it too. And I'm never going to receive the test answers. It's all just a scam. And why not? Who am I going to tell? I can just imagine going to my parents, the police, or the school and telling them that Dirk the Dirtbag tricked me into paying him for exam answers and then took off with my money. Yeah, right.

The first thing I do is go to the bathroom and wash my hands, over and over, with soap and water. I want to take a shower too. To wash away the nasty filth it feels like I just rolled in. Will I ever be clean again? As I'm drying my hands, I remember that God is the only one who can make me truly clean. It's Jesus who washes away my sin.

But as quickly as this thought hits me, I swipe it away. In order to be cleansed like that, I'd have to confess my sin and ask for forgiveness . . . and I'm just not ready to have that conversation yet. In fact, I haven't spoken to God since last Friday . . . since I cheated in AP Biology.

I go to my room and turn on my computer, going immediately to e-mail, where there are no messages with the subject "Better Yourself" anywhere. And I am relieved. Maybe this really is a scam. And I deserve to be scammed. Really, it would be a relief . . . and an end to this nasty business. Sure, I'm going down and my lackluster GPA might even ruin my chances at Stanford, but at least I'd be done with this. And who knows, maybe I could still get into another school. I've heard that UCLA has good med programs. And there's always my parents' alma mater, USC.

Despite my twisted hope that I've been scammed, I keep checking my e-mail. I know I should be studying, but I'm too distracted and distraught. So I play Spider Solitaire and check my e-mail.

"Hey, GraceAnn," my dad calls into my room, making me jump. "Come help me make dinner."

I close my laptop and go out to lend a hand, trying to act natural as he makes small talk and I make a salad. Then my mom comes home, and we sit down at the table together. If anyone was looking on, they would assume we were a sweet little family. No one would even guess there was a lying cheater among us.

"Aren't you hungry?" Dad asks as he notices I've barely touched my food.

I shrug. "I guess not."

"I thought you liked my pesto pasta."

"I usually do." I give him a weak smile. "Sorry."

"You're not coming down with something?" Mom peers at me with a creased brow.

"I think I'm just preoccupied with studying. Remember, it's finals week."

"That's right." Dad reaches for my plate. "Maybe you should get back to it. I'll do cleanup tonight."

I thank him and excuse myself, but as I go to my room, I feel even guiltier than before. I wish Mom and Dad weren't being so supportive and understanding. Especially considering how I've compromised myself. If my parents had any idea what I've been up to or why I'm so eager to get back to my room, I can't even imagine how they'd react.

But don't they understand that at the same time they're being so nicey-nice, they are also putting a lot of demands on me? Expecting me to bring home stellar grades, a perfect GPA, get into the best college—even Harvard for Pete's sake—and then play softball in the springtime.

Oh, I'm not trying to blame my parents for my bad choices . . . but maybe if they were more like Mary Beth's mom—more laid back and without so many high expecta-tions—maybe I wouldn't be in this position right now. Don't parents know what kind of pressure we get at school? Don't they care?

I check my e-mail again and am surprised to see something new. And the subject heading, just like Dirk promised, says "Better Yourself." My heart begins to pound as I open the e-mail. All it says is: "Here you go."

I move the cursor to the first attachment, which is just numbers and letters. My hand freezes and I'm concerned about opening it. What if this really is a bad trick? What if I open this doc and my whole computer gets infected with a killer virus and goes into a meltdown? Or what if Dirk is actually an undercover cop and I'm about to get arrested for cheating? Do people get arrested for cheating? I don't think so. Still, I feel sick with apprehension. What on earth am I doing?

Those words start running through my mind again: *every-one does it, everyone does it, everyone does it.*

Then without giving it another thought, I open the first attachment. It turns out to be instructions on how to load the second attachment onto my calculator. I read it carefully, several times, and before long, I'm actually downloading the program. Like Dirk said, it's easy. And when I experiment with it, I find that it actually works. Just like the explanation says it will.

I open the third doc and am surprised that it not only contains the answers to the exam but the exam itself. I read over the questions and am convinced this is the right test because it covers pretty much everything we've studied over the past several months. I consider simply trying to memorize the answers, but then decide to go with the bracelet technique again. Just to be safe.

Do I feel good about any of this? Of course not. I feel like a criminal and a hypocrite, and my only consolation is that I will never, ever do this again. As I'm printing test answers, I blame Clayton for this. If I hadn't fallen so hard for him, if I hadn't been so heartbroken when he dumped me, I never would've ended up in this position. And I promise myself that I will never put myself in a position like that with a guy again. From now on, school will come first.

And even though Bryant's a nice guy and I really do like him, I will not let him get to me like I let Clayton. I have learned my lesson the hard way, and right now I'm paying the price. All I want is to get through this week — and to put it behind me.

With my cheating documents safely stored and printed, I dump and dispose of the e-mail trail and start studying for the AP History exam I have tomorrow afternoon. Fortunately, this is a class I'm already strong in. I have a solid A so far in there, and unless I fall apart tomorrow, I should have this one in the bag. Even so, I study until eleven just to be sure.

As I get ready for bed, I wish that grades weren't this important. I pick up a trophy I won for a spelling bee in fifth grade and wish that I could be ten years old and innocent again. Back then it was easy and natural to excel at school. I didn't even have to try very hard. Back then I never would've resorted to something as disgraceful as cheating. Life was so much simpler before . . . before now.

Have I sealed my fate—will it ever be like that again?

## CHAPTER 10

**I** don't see why you're so worried about finals this time," Mary Beth says to me as we're going into the school. "Just remember all the times you've sailed through them. Focus on the positive more . . . maybe it'll help."

"Thanks." I force a smile. She has no idea why I'm so bummed, and I have no intention of disclosing it to her. "I'll keep that in mind."

"Good luck," she calls as I head toward the math department.

I used my super antiperspirant this morning — the brand I usually reserve for things like softball games or scary social events. Even so, as I walk into the classroom, I can feel myself sweating. And my palms are damp. My stomach hurts and my heart is already racing like I just ran the mile. The way my body is reacting to all this makes me understand how people fail lie-detector tests.

I take the same seat as yesterday — after I saw the F on my weekly test. Hopefully Mr. VanDorssen won't notice or care that I'm not sitting up near the front like I used to. I wonder if I'll even want to sit in front in this class again. Will I ever get past this day and go back to normal? Is there such a thing as normal?

The last bell rings and, wasting no time, I begin the exam. Following instructions as usual, I am equipped with only my calculator and a number-two pencil. I'm still doubtful that this program is really going to work. What if Dirk got the answers for the wrong test? Would I even care? But as I begin the first problem, I can tell I have the right program. It matches. And I slowly work my way through all of them, taking what seems an adequate amount of time for each one and filling in the appropriate answers at regular intervals. I begin to relax just a little. And I remember that everyone else is doing the same thing. Well, except for a few unsuspecting students who, like me, will have to figure this out the hard way. Life is unfair. And that's just how it is.

As I hand in my paper, I feel Mr. VanDorssen's eyes on me, lingering a little longer than usual. "How did it go, Miss Lowery?"

"Okay, I think." I flash him a nervous smile. "It felt like I was on top of my game."

He nods. "Good to know."

Then I leave and, feeling slightly numb and empty, slowly walk to the cafeteria. We get a full hour for lunch break during finals week, and usually it's a time for kids to let their hair down and enjoy the extra time. But I just wish the hands on the clock would turn faster.

"Still obsessing over yesterday's bad grade?" Bryant asks as he joins Mary Beth and me.

"No," I tell him. "I'm beyond that."

"So how did your final go?"

"Okay." I try to brighten my countenance. I know my friends can't enjoy hanging with such a downer. "How was your test?" I ask him.

Bryant tells about how it was an essay test, which he usually hates. "But today I was really pushing myself to try harder." He grins at me. "I guess you're a good influence on me."

I swallow the bite of cheeseburger I've barely chewed, feeling the hard lump moving slowly down my esophagus and wondering if I'm going to choke on it. I reach for my soda and take a gulp from my straw.

Fortunately, Mary Beth changes the subject by complaining about the test she just suffered through in French class, going on about how she'll probably never graduate if she can't successfully finish just one year of a language.

"You should let me tutor you in French," Jorge tells her.

"You're good in French?" She blinks.

"Good enough."

"Jorge's already taken three years of it," Bryant brags.

Jorge shrugs. "I'm a teaching assistant in Mrs. Klausner's fifth period."

"I didn't know that." Mary Beth's eyes literally have stars in them now.

Once again I leave the table early. I'm sure my friends wonder about me. Maybe they assume I have some sort of stomach ailment. As a matter of fact, I'm not so sure that I don't. But I feel so antsy that I just can't sit there another minute. I wonder if I'll get ulcers.

Eventually the first bell rings and I go to AP History. I'm early, but this is not so unusual for me. Before long, I'm taking the final and feeling like I really am in my zone. I wouldn't say the test is easy, but I do feel prepared for it. And I'll be surprised if I don't get an A. But the best part is the feeling of achievement I have when I turn it in. Like I did this on my own — no help needed. I wish it was like that for all my classes.

. . . . . . . . . .

The next day of finals passes without incident or too much stress . . . probably because there's no cheating involved on my part. I can't be certain about everyone else. I suppose my own experience is making me more cynical about others. I might even be worried about how their illicit activities might hinder my grades, but I feel quite secure in these two classes and am therefore unconcerned.

As a result, I feel more relaxed at the end of the day, like I'm almost starting to feel comfortable in my own skin again. Except that I know the AP Biology final still lurks before me. As I go into the house after school, I'm painfully aware that my short life of crime is not over. How I wish it were.

I go directly to my room and begin to work on my cheating bracelet. I plan to be even more clever than Kelsey with this. I'm using a real bracelet as camouflage. I select a silver bangle that is just the right width to conceal the strip of paper I printed and cut to fit. I'm just securing the paper with tape when someone taps on my door.

I shove the bracelet onto my wrist. "Who is it?"

"Just me, honey," Mom calls. "Can I come in?"

I push the paper scraps, tape, and scissors into my desk drawer. "Sure," I call out.

"What's up?" she asks as she comes into my room and looks around.

"Just studying."

"That's what I thought."

"You're home early."

She stretches her neck from side to side. "Slow day at the hospital. And I've gotten so much overtime lately that I decided to leave."

"Oh . . ." I nod, fiddling with my bracelet.

"Anyway, Dad called and told me to ask you about how set you were for winter wear."

"Winter wear?" I frown. "You mean like mittens and things? It's not like we need a lot of that around here."

She shrugs. "I know. I wasn't too sure what he meant either." She goes over to my closet. "Mind if I look around?"

"No." I go over to join her. "What are we looking for?" Suddenly I feel worried. Does she know something? Did she somehow find out about what I've done? But why would she be looking in my closet?

She pulls out an old parka. "Does this still fit you?"

"I guess."

She pokes around some more, and I start to think she's really only looking for winter wear like she said. Still, it's weird. "Okay." She turns back and smiles. "I'll tell him we're fairly well set."

"Do you think he's going to take us somewhere cold?"

"That's a good guess. But let's just play dumb. I can tell he's got something up his sleeve, and you know how your dad loves to catch us off guard."

I nod. "The King of Surprise."

"Okay, I'll let you get back to your studying." She yawns. "And I plan to take a nice long, hot bath."

"Enjoy," I call as she leaves.

As soon as the door closes, I slip off the bracelet and just stare at it. What if my mom found out about this stupid bracelet? What if my parents knew how low I've sunk? Would it be worth the humiliation? Without cheating I might still get a C for my final grade. Well, unless I get an F on the final exam, which seems likely considering I haven't studied like I should.

An F will drop my overall grade down to a solid D. I just cannot afford a D.

It feels like my fate is sealed. I have to finish what I started. But when I'm done, I will never, ever do this again. I swear to myself I won't.

· · · · · · · · · ·

As I walk into AP Biology, wearing my silver cheater's bracelet, I am filled with despair and self-loathing. Still, I see no way out of this mess I've created. *Just get it over and done with.*

Kelsey is sitting at the table across from me. Her cheater's bracelet is not easy to spot this time because she's wearing a white shirt and the white strip of paper is neatly tucked within the cuff, but as soon as she starts the test, I notice her occasionally scratching, changing positions, fidgeting.

All of this is pretty normal test behavior, and as I glance around the room, I can see that others are doing likewise. I look down at my own paper. Is everyone wearing a cheater's bracelet? Or do some people use other means? In the instructions doc Dirk sent me, there was a whole list of ways to cheat. Some of them seemed pretty ridiculous, not to mention tricky.

But the silver bracelet works for me. And by the end of the class, I neatly fill in the last answer and then sit up straight to stretch my spine. As I do this, I catch Kelsey staring at me with a knowing look. Like she observed me cheating. Of course, this could be my guilty imagination. But as she gives me a sly smile, I'm sure that she's aware. I just hope no one else noticed.

I glance up to where Ms. Bannister is sitting at her desk, checking her iPhone with an absent expression. And then the release bell rings and everyone starts filing up to her desk to turn in their exams.

I avoid her eyes as I set mine on top of the others. Then, worried that this could make me appear guiltier, I look directly at her and smile. "Have a good Christmas," I say lightly.

"Thanks, GraceAnn. You too."

Feeling like some of the weight has been lifted from my back, I leave the room. *You can relax now. It's all over, and it's time to get back to your life.*

But just then Kelsey comes along, walking beside me. "I see you met Dirk," she says in a sassy tone.

I just shrug.

"I *saw* you cheating," she hisses into my ear. "I can't believe what a hypocrite you are, GraceAnn. Acting like you're so much better than the rest of us, but the truth is, you're no different. Except that you're a hypocrite."

I turn to face her. "It's because of people like you that I had to do what I did. You mess up the grading curve and ruin — "

"We all have our little excuses now, don't we?" She gives me a smug look. "Maybe you won't be so quick to judge next time." Then she skips off on her merry little way, probably imagining herself behind the wheel of the Mustang her stepdad is going to give her for pulling an A in an AP class. Well, whatever!

I try to shake this off as I go into the cafeteria. I'm determined to act like everything is just fine. And really, it is fine. Except that I feel dirty inside and I wonder what it'll take to get clean again. Also, Kelsey's words keep ringing in my ears. She's right . . . I am a hypocrite.

"Only a week until Christmas," Mary Beth announces to our lunch table as we settle in to eat. "Anybody doing anything exciting during the break?"

"I agreed to work at my aunt's restaurant while my uncle

recovers from surgery," Jorge says a bit glumly. "Now I'm wishing I hadn't."

"Well, at least you'll be making some money," Bryant tells him. "Not to mention eating well."

"I think my dad might have a surprise up his sleeve." Then I tell them about the mysterious question over winter wear.

"Maybe you're going to a ski resort for winter break," Bryant suggests.

"I thought about that. Except my parents' work schedules are usually too busy for them to get away for more than a day at a time."

We visit and eat and visit some more, and by the time lunch ends, I almost feel like my old self again. Almost. We wish each other luck with our next finals and go our separate ways. But I'm feeling confident about journalism this year. Compared to trig and AP Biology, it's a walk in the park.

By the time school lets out, I think I might actually survive my self-inflicted ordeal. Oh, I'm certainly not proud of what I've pulled off. But it was a way to get by. In the long run, when I'm going to Stanford, it'll all be worth it. Really, a girl's got to do what a girl's got to do.

"Want to go out and celebrate?" I ask Mary Beth as we're walking to the car. "I'll spot you for a mocha."

"Seems a little early to celebrate," she says in a dismal tone. "We still have tomorrow's finals to slog through."

"Yes, but it's just art. That's a no-brainer."

"I'm not talking about art." She lets out a groan. "I asked to retake my algebra final."

"Why?"

"Because I know I blew it on Tuesday. And Mr. Johnson has a one-time-only retake policy, which I plan to exercise. So I'm not ready to celebrate just yet. I need to go home and study."

"Okay."

"You seem to be feeling a lot less stressed," she says as I pull up to her house.

"Yeah . . ." I let out a sigh. "I'll be so glad to have this week behind me."

"I know. I was actually starting to get worried."

"About your finals?"

"No. About you. You haven't been yourself at all, GraceAnn. I was worried that you were losing it. But you do seem better now." She peers curiously at me. "Do you think you did okay on your tests?"

I nod. "Yeah, I think so. Like you said, I just needed to think more positively and relax a little."

"Now I just need to take my own advice." She grimaces as she reaches for her bag. "That algebra final could undo me."

"You'll be fine."

"Easy for you to say. You're ready to go out and celebrate. My graduating hinges on some of these classes."

For one crazy moment, I am tempted to tell her about Dirk. Naturally, I do not. That would be insane. Not only is he too expensive for Mary Beth, it's just wrong. I can't even imagine how shocked she'd be if I mentioned it to her. Or what she would say if she knew that I'd already gone to him . . . already cheated. I don't even want to think about it.

Instead, I tell her not to study too hard. "And don't stay up too late," I call out. "That always messes you up more than it helps."

As she's waving and walking toward her house, my cell phone rings. To my surprise, it's Dirk. "So, how did it go?" he asks with way too much familiarity.

"It went okay," I say carefully.

"No problems, then?"

"No." Now I'm feeling uneasy with my car still parked in front of Mary Beth's house. And although it's illegal, I put my car into gear with the phone still by my ear and slowly drive down the block, then park again.

"Well, I'm glad to hear that, GraceAnn. Glad I could help you out."

"And I appreciate it." Suddenly I'm feeling nervous again. Like this really isn't over yet. And I want to ask him why he's calling me out of the blue like this. Is this some kind of customer service he offers?

"And you remember I told you that you'd owe me one, right?"

I feel the pit of my stomach twisting. "I told you, I don't think I know anyone to send your way."

"And that's okay. That's not what I'm calling about."

"Then what?" I hate to even think of what a dirtbag guy like Dirk might possibly want from me. And it sickens me to think that he has any right to expect anything. What if I just told him to get lost and hung up the phone?

"I want you to pick me up some OxyContin at work."

"What?" I screech into the phone.

"You heard me. And then we'll be even."

"Are you nuts?" Now I'm not an expert at the pharmacy, but I know that OxyContin is a highly addictive pain med and is extremely valuable to pill peddlers.

"No, GraceAnn. I'm not nuts. I just need you to nab me some OxyContin. No big deal. I'm sure there's plenty of it at your pharmacy."

"First of all, it's not *my* pharmacy. Second of all, my uncle keeps that kind of thing locked up in a secure area."

"Well, it can't *always* be locked up. And I'm sure you know how to get to it if you want—"

"Even if I *could* do that, there is no way on God's green earth I *would* do that, Dirk. So you might as well get that through your—"

"Hold on there," he says in a strangely calm voice. "It's up to you whether or not you get it for me. But like I said, you *owe* me. And if you refuse to pay up, I have other ways of getting even with you."

"What other ways?"

"First of all, I'll let the school know you cheated."

"How?"

He laughs. "It's easy. I just send them a copy of what I sent you. They check your tests and the evidence is all there. And it won't be the first time I've pulled the plug on a customer who let me down."

"But what if I get you the rest of the money?" Suddenly $250 more doesn't sound like such a steep price. "I could have it to you by—"

"The problem is that I'm not in need of money right now. But I could use some OxyContin. And I thought you were just the girl to get it for me, GraceAnn. Guess I was wrong."

"But it's Christmas break and my family is going on vacation." Okay, this is another big fat lie, but it's all I have. And besides, it's Dirtbag I'm talking to. Not a real person. "So anyway, I'm not even scheduled to work until after the New Year and—"

"Okay, fine," he snaps. "I'll give you a couple of weeks to get it for me. But don't think I'm letting you off the hook. I expect to be paid in full in January. If you let me down, I'll make your life miserable. Understand?"

"Yeah," I mutter. "I understand."

If I thought my life was messed up before, it is way beyond that now. What I thought was an endless black hole, swallowing me alive, is starting to feel more like hell. The nastiest sort of hell—because it's a place I helped to create with my own two hands, and now it threatens to drag others down into it with me. I'm beginning to feel that there is no escape.

## CHAPTER 11

"**I** get why Mary Beth is so agitated," Bryant says to me at the lunch table on Friday. "She still has that algebra final. But what's up with you?"

"Nothing." I set down the soda can I've been fidgeting with and fake a carefree expression. "Just restless is all."

"You should be feeling pretty good by now." Mary Beth frowns at me. "Or are you still worrying about your grades?"

"I'm not worried," I say in a slightly irate tone.

Her brows arch. "Okay then." She glances at Jorge, and he just shrugs.

"Hey, I have an idea," he says. "Why don't we all go out tonight to celebrate? There are a couple of new movies just out and —"

"I can't," Mary Beth says with disappointment. "I promised my mom I'd go Christmas shopping with her tonight."

"How about tomorrow?" he asks eagerly.

Her eyes light up. "Tomorrow works."

"How about you guys?" He nods to Bryant.

"Sure, I'm game, but I can't speak for GraceAnn."

The truth is, I don't really want to go out with them. Not because I don't like them, but because I feel like crawling under a rock somewhere. "I have to work tomorrow," I say absently, like that's an excuse.

"But you get off at five," Mary Beth says.

"I know . . ." I shrug. "But if you wanted to go early . . ."

"Not that early." Jorge is checking his iPhone and starts listing off movie titles and showtimes. Before I know it, I've reluctantly agreed to go with them and will be picked up at six thirty.

Now the first bell rings, and as Mary Beth stands, her face looks like she's on her way to an execution. "Wish me luck."

"You'll do fine," I assure her. "Just relax . . . and don't forget to breathe."

Bryant laughs. "You should take your own advice, Lowery."

I glare at him. Besides the slam, it's the first time he's called me by my last name in a while, and he knows I don't like it.

He holds his hands up innocently. "Just kidding."

Ignoring him, I tell Mary Beth to meet me in the parking lot when she's done with her final.

"Or I can give her a ride home," Jorge offers with hopeful dark eyes. This guy's got it bad for her. And although he's sweet, I wonder if she's really getting serious about him — and for some reason that troubles me. But it's too late. She's already agreeing to this new plan.

"Maybe GraceAnn can give you a ride home," Jorge says to Bryant. "Unless you want to stick around and wait for us."

"Do you mind?" Bryant asks me.

Well, it so happens that I do mind, but I suspect I'm acting like a spoiled brat, so I smile and say, "No problem."

"I need to get some stuff from the locker room. Do you minding waiting a few minutes?" he asks.

I agree to this, and as I'm checking my phone, Kelsey passes by. She gives me another one of her smug smiles, and without thinking, I stand up and call out to her. Suddenly I'm curious about something, but as I walk over, I wonder what I'll actually say to her.

"*What?*" she says in a grumpy tone, like I'm not worth her time.

"How much do you know about Dirk Zimmerman?" I quietly ask. There are still a few students lingering in the cafeteria.

"Why?" She tilts her head to one side with narrowed eyes.

"Has he ever threatened you?"

"What do you mean?" She glances around like she's worried someone might be eavesdropping, but no one's close enough to hear us.

"I *mean* he's a low-life blackmailer."

Her eyes get bigger. "What are you talking about?"

"I'm talking about what a jerk he is. And I wish you'd never told me about the lying bottom-feeder."

Now she looks aggravated. "Hey, you *made* me tell you. I didn't want to. So if he's jerking you around, that's your problem."

"So he never jerks you around?"

She gives me a catty smile. "Dirk *likes* me."

"Right." I can see it now. She probably bats those big blue eyes at him, talks real sweet, and she's got him eating out of her hand. Problem is, I don't have that same kind of charm.

"You probably just rubbed him wrong. You're not exactly Miss Congeniality, you know."

I roll my eyes. "So he's never threatened you at all? Never tried to get more money out of you?"

She shakes her head.

Suddenly I'm wondering, at $250 a pop for test answers, how can she possibly manage to afford it? "Well, you must be rich."

"Huh?"

"Because I was just doing the math, and if you've been buying test answers from him all term to secure that A, it would cost around $1,500."

She looks shocked. "No way. I never paid anything close to that."

"How much was it?"

She folds her arms across her front. "Why should I tell you? I don't even know why I'm talking to you in the first place. It's not like we're friends."

"I'm just curious." I try to soften my tone and force a smile. "I mean, it's kind of like we're in this together, aren't we?"

She looks dubious. "Why don't you tell me how much you paid?"

I consider this. Really, what difference does it make? "Well, he was going to charge me $250." I'm not going to mention I had to buy for two finals. The less this girl knows, the better I'll feel. "But since it was my first time, he cut it in half. At the time I thought he was being generous, but now—"

"You paid $250 for one test?" She laughs. "That's *way* more than what he normally charges. Sounds like he *really* doesn't like you, GraceAnn."

I'm trying to wrap my head around this. "So what does he usually charge?"

"I don't know why I'm telling you. Except maybe to rub it in. Dirk gave me a package deal. All the answers for AP Biology for $300." She grins. "And getting a Mustang for that price seems like a pretty good deal to me."

I cannot believe it. But she has no reason to lie about it.

"Too bad for you, GraceAnn. I guess you smart kids aren't so smart after all." She laughs as she walks away. And I just stand there, probably with my mouth hanging open.

"What were you two talking about?" Bryant asks.

I blink and try to act natural. "Nothing."

"Kelsey seemed pretty amused about something." He frowns at me. "And you look like you're not feeling well. Everything okay?"

"Everything's just peachy," I growl as I shove my arms in the sleeves of my jacket.

His brows arch. "Somebody having a bad day?"

I grab up my stuff, telling myself to calm down. "Sorry. I guess I'm just in a bad mood."

"Was it something Kelsey said to you?" he asks as we walk out together.

"I guess so." Now I'm trying to think of some kind of explanation.

"Isn't she the one you suspected of cheating the other day? Did you confront her on it or something?"

I just nod.

"Well, she doesn't seem too worried," he continues. "Did she claim to be innocent?"

"Well, it's not like she was going to give me her full confession."

"So what did you say to her? Did you read her the riot act? Did you tell her she's making it hard on you?"

"Something like that." I sigh.

He pats me on the back as we walk to the parking lot. "At least you have the satisfaction of knowing you're doing things right, GraceAnn. Besides that, you're actually getting an education while Kelsey is buying it. That alone should make you feel good."

How I wish I felt good. But as he continues to talk about what an inspiration I am to him and how his whole attitude toward school is changing, my stomach twists and turns and I wish he would just shut up. *Just shut up.*

"Sorry I'm not very chatty," I tell him as I start my car. "I've got this nasty headache." That is actually true. My head is throbbing.

We don't say much as I drive him home. He lives in a subdivision a few miles from my house. It's one of those developments where all the houses look the same, and I wonder if people ever get lost trying to find their way home.

"Thanks," he says as he gets out. "Sorry you're not feeling well. Hope you're not coming down with something."

I give him a weak smile. "Me too."

But as I drive home, I wish I was coming down with something—something serious . . . perhaps even something lethal. To escape my problems, I climb into bed. I want to go to sleep . . . and stay asleep for about a year. I wish I could go into a coma.

When my parents get home, they invite me to go out to dinner with them, but I say I'm not feeling well.

"Maybe we should stay home with you," Mom says. "It seems like you've been under the weather a lot lately." Now she starts to talk like a doctor, asking me all the usual medical questions.

"Stop worrying," I finally tell her. "It's nothing serious. I just want to get some rest."

"Maybe you should call in sick tomorrow," Dad suggests.

I nod. "Yeah, I might do that." And I want to add that I might call in sick for the rest of my senior year too.

"Make sure you're drinking plenty of fluids," Mom says. "And just call us if you need anything."

"I know, I know."

"How about if I heat you up some chicken noodle soup?" Dad offers.

"Yeah, that sounds good. But I can do it myself." I feel guilty with them treating me like this, caring so much . . . and knowing how I don't deserve it.

"No." Dad shakes his head. "It's the least I can do."

"You go back to bed," Mom tells me. "Just relax."

"And I'll bring it to you," Dad calls out as he heads for the kitchen.

I don't protest, but feeling even more miserable and guilty, I shuffle back to my room and crawl into bed. I hate myself. Even Rory is looking at me with what seem like suspicious eyes. Or maybe he's just pouting because I haven't taken him on a walk for days.

Before long, Dad appears with a tray. He's heated a generous bowl of soup, poured a tall glass of orange juice, and even added some cheese and crackers. "Here you go, princess." He sets it on my lap, then pats me on the head. "You be sure to call us if you feel any worse."

I nod, quietly thanking him. Then I poke at my food, realizing that everything has seemed kind of tasteless today. Perhaps I really am getting sick. After my parents leave, I let Rory finish the soup in my bowl as I get out of bed. I start pacing back and forth in my room, but Rory thinks I want to play. So I go out and prowl about the darkened house.

At first Rory follows me around. I'm sure he thinks I've lost my mind. In some ways, I'm sure that I have. But I'm hoping this activity will somehow wake up my brain and help me figure out a plan—some kind of answer to my ever-growing heap of trouble.

A small part of me—that quiet voice that is probably

coming from God—is saying, "Just come clean, GraceAnn. Confess what you did, take the consequences, and never do it again." It sounds so simple . . . and tempting. Really, isn't that the best way out? Come clean?

But for the life of me, I cannot imagine actually doing this. How can I possibly tell everyone that I'm a liar and a cheat? What will my parents say? My friends? My teachers? My whole life, for as long as I can remember, has been highlighted by my academic achievements. My scholastic superiority. I've always gotten positive attention for my outstanding grades. And I liked it. How can I possibly let that all go down the drain? Especially after working so hard for all these years? It's like I've been blind-sided, and I don't understand how it's possible to lose everything all because of two little tests. How is that even fair?

And what about Stanford? What if I confessed about cheating and it went on my permanent record and ruined all my chances of going to Stanford? Perhaps it would ruin my chances for any college. I have no idea how seriously something like this could be taken, and I don't even know how to find out. It's not like I can go in and ask the dean about what happens when you get caught cheating. Talk about a red flag.

Next I go over my conversation with Kelsey. I'm still fuming that Dirk gave her such a good deal. How is that fair? Then I realize how ridiculous it is for me to think about Dirk the Dirtbag in terms of fairness. He makes the rules and breaks the rules. He doesn't have to play fair, and he knows it. I am at a distinct disadvantage.

Even so, I'm an intelligent person—or I used to be—and I really should be able to come up with some kind of escape plan. Like what if I confronted Dirk and threatened to expose his nasty little cheating business? Blackmail the blackmailer?

I wonder how I could make my story sound legit. Maybe I could tell him that my conscience has gotten the best of me and I plan to go forward and confess everything. And then I could claim that if he doesn't stop his blackmail attempts, I will use him as my bargaining chip in an attempt to minimize my own consequences. Kind of like a plea bargain. What would he say to that? Would he back down? Could we come to a congenial agreement?

But then I remember that sinister look in his eyes. I remember his severe warning—that others have tried to take him down and suffered consequences. And obviously he's still around and still doing business, which seems to back up his claims. But is he really infallible? There must be some way to make a guy like that tumble. He certainly deserves to be brought down. And wouldn't I love to be the one to do it.

Except that bringing him down will almost certainly mean that I go down too. And I'm just not ready for that. Not if I can help it. As I pace back and forth, I decide that I will not go down. Not without a good fight.

I consider the Dirtbag's demands now—that I get him some OxyContin. It's hard to believe that one small bottle of those innocent-looking little pills could buy my freedom. It just doesn't see equitable. It's like those pills could save my life.

I know my aunt and uncle love me and would support me in most things. However, they would not support me in something like this. They would be thoroughly shocked and disappointed to know I'd even consider such a thing. And really, I'm not considering it. Not seriously. I'm just going over everything bit by bit, trying to analyze my options and come up with some kind of plan—some way out.

Now I start to rationalize. What if I could do something for my aunt and uncle to make up for sneaking the pain pills? I would gladly offer to babysit Ben and Tim, their bratty four-year-old twins, for free. Those preschoolers are a royal pain, but I would happily watch them for a week just to get out of this prison I've built. Not that I can exactly trade pills for babysitting.

How much does a bottle of OxyContin really cost? Probably not much since Uncle Russ buys everything in bulk and at wholesale prices. The markup on some drugs is huge; that's how he turns a profit. But even though the street value on pain meds is crazy high, it's not like they charge a fortune for people with legitimate prescriptions. I'll bet those pills cost less than a dollar a piece. And if there were thirty in the prescription, I could slip thirty dollars into the till when no one was looking. Or would that be too weird?

That I'm even thinking about all this, actually considering doing what I know is breaking the law, is extremely disturbing. Who am I? What have I become? But at the same time, I know that if I don't think it all through, I'll never figure my way out.

Finally my brain feels tired, and my bare feet are cold and sore from walking back and forth over the hard tile floor. It feels like my mind is spinning in circles, and nothing seems to make any sense at all. I have no plan. So feeling defeated, I go to bed in the hopes that I can escape myself for a while.

But when morning comes, I get up with this weird but specific kind of clarity. Like I made the decision during my sleep. Although I actually made it around three in the morning when I was lying there wide awake. It all seemed crystal clear . . . and doable.

I've decided that the only way to end this thing is to simply steal the pills, give them to Dirk, and then I'll quit my job. I'll make up some good excuse for my parents and aunt and uncle, like I need more time to devote to my studies. That's believable.

In fact, after this term, I can see that it's true.

Then after I hand over the pills, I will tell Dirk that I got fired. I'll even make it look like it's his fault because I've been suspected of stealing. But I won't act like I'm mad at him. My thinking is if he knows I'm not working there anymore, he can't blackmail me for more pills. And maybe he'll assume I don't have any money either. And if I get really lucky, he might even feel a tiny bit sorry for me.

Also, I'll make it clear that since I'm now unemployed, my finances are so tight that I won't be able to purchase any more test answers. But I'll do all this in a very sweet and congenial way. I'll even thank him for "helping" me. Kelsey had hinted that if I was nicer to Dirk, he might be nicer to me.

Somehow I have got to shake this creep off. And I figure if he doesn't see me as his free pass to illegally gotten prescription drugs, he might lose all interest in me. I can only hope.

## CHAPTER 12

"**Y**ou must be feeling better," Mom says to me as I come into the kitchen fully dressed in the morning.

"Yeah." I fill a commuter cup with coffee. "I'm fine."

"That's a relief. I started to think of all the things you could be suffering from last night."

"Just one of the perks of practicing medicine?"

She grins. "I guess so."

"Anyway, since I'm not contagious or anything, I'm going to work."

"Oh, that reminds me. Last night Dad said you should tell Uncle Russ that you need next Saturday off."

I nod. "Oh, that must have something to do with his winter clothes question."

She grins as she pours cream into her coffee. "Yes, but we'll pretend we don't know, okay?"

"Sure." Now I lower my voice. "Do you think he's taking us to play in the snow for the day?"

"I hope so." She takes a sip of her coffee and sighs. "I've been dreaming of real snow lately."

I give her a sympathetic smile. My mom spent most of her childhood in Minnesota, so she sometimes gets like this. "Oh, by the way, I have a date tonight," I tell her.

She smiles. "That's nice. Is it with Bryant?"

I nod as I stir sugar into my cup.

"I like him. He seems like a genuinely nice boy."

I shrug and put the lid on my cup. "I guess so."

"What do you mean, you guess so?"

I take a test sip of my coffee. "Well, after what happened with Clayton, I'll make sure not to get too involved with a guy. I'd rather focus on my studies."

She seems to consider this, then slowly nods. "Sounds like a wise plan."

I take an apple out of the fruit bowl and shove it in my jacket pocket. "Yeah, that's what I thought too."

"Even so, you can be friends with him," she calls as I head out. "No harm in that."

I yell good-bye and hurry out to my car. The wind is blowing and it's starting to rain. Not exactly the snow Mom is wishing for, but it does feel a bit more like winter. And it fits my mood better too.

I turn up my stereo, hoping to block out my thoughts with music. I don't want to think about what's going down today. I don't want to obsess over what I plan to do. I'd like to imagine that I'm simply sleepwalking or a zombie, just going through the paces . . . and then I want to forget about it.

That's probably because I rehearsed the whole thing, over and over, in my head last night. I woke up at three and realized I needed to get it down. As a result I'm wearing a hoodie today. One with deep, thick pockets. The plan is that the first time I see any OxyContin out — and if no one is around to see — I will walk past and pocket it. After that, I'll go clean the bathroom, and then I'll transfer the loose pills into my jeans pocket. I wore a looser-fitting pair of jeans expressly for this purpose, so no one will see the outline of pills in my pocket.

Then I will thoroughly cleanse (to avoid fingerprints) and dispose of the pill bottle, wrapping it in toilet paper like it's a used tampon. If someone else finds it later, which I think is unlikely, it won't matter. It will simply appear that a customer snatched it and emptied it in there. The trash won't be taken out until tomorrow.

I had considered taking some kind of substitute pills to work, switching them for actual OxyContin pills, and then giving them to the customer. But that worries me. What if the customer really needed them . . . and became sicker . . . and came back and sued my aunt and uncle? I couldn't live with that. This way just seems simpler. And it does seem feasible that someone could sneak in and snatch a prescription from the high counter where they are placed when finished. Of course, it would have to be a tall person.

And thankfully, although he talks about it all the time, my uncle hasn't installed a real surveillance camera. He has a good fake one up and is under the impression that it keeps crooks at bay. But after today, he might want to invest in the real thing. And I don't think that's a bad idea.

My heart is pounding hard as I go into the pharmacy, but I'm ready with a smile and a greeting. My aunt, decked out in a red-and-white Santa hat and completely oblivious to the diabolical plan up my sleeve, greets me back, telling me how my young cousins sneakily unwrapped a couple of the presents from beneath the tree.

She laughs. "Good thing their gifts were still stashed in the attic. All they got was a shirt for grandpa and a tool set for Russ. Then they tried to rewrap them. Like I wouldn't notice. When

I brought it to their attention, saying that I have eyes in the back of my head, they almost seemed to believe me."

I make a nervous laugh. "Yeah, I remember when my mom used to give me that line too. Eventually we figure it out."

"Just wait until you're a mom. You'll use it too." She hands me a Santa hat. "Here, let's be festive."

Just as I'm putting it on, the phone rings and a customer comes in. It seems the morning has officially begun. Since it's full-blown flu season now, there are more customers than usual, and it takes a while before I can take a breath, get my bearings, and remember my plan.

Of course, it now occurs to me that there's always the chance no one will bring in a prescription for OxyContin today. Although I doubt it. I think it's one of the more common prescriptions. It's like all the doctors are prescribing it.

And sure enough, around eleven a customer comes in with a prescription for it. "It's probably going to be about an hour," I quietly tell her. This isn't true, but it buys me time. "Do you have other shopping to do?"

"I sure do." She pulls out a list. "With Christmas less than a week away, who doesn't?"

I smile and hand her a candy cane. "Here. In case you get low blood sugar."

She laughs and thanks me. "I just might need that."

I keep myself busy, which isn't hard to do, and after about thirty minutes, I see what I'm sure is the OxyContin prescription appear on the high shelf. But I go past a couple of times, looking closely, just to be sure. Meanwhile I wait on customers and try not to sweat.

Finally it's getting close to lunchtime, and I'm worried that I'm going to miss my opportunity. But Aunt Lindsey is still working away and in full view of the shelf so there's no way I can nab it without risking being noticed.

"I'm going to lunch in a few minutes," I remind her, "in case you need a bathroom break first."

"Oh, good idea. Thanks."

And just like that she's gone. With trembling hands, I walk past the shelf, glancing around to be sure no one is looking my way, and in one swift move, I snag the bottle and tuck it into my pocket. As I walk back over to the cash register, it feels like I'm about to have a heart attack. My heart is racing and it feels like I can hardly breathe. I hope I won't pass out. How would I explain the pills in my pocket?

"Where's the first-aid aisle?" a middle-aged woman asks me. I try to calm myself as I lead her over, helping her find just the right elastic bandage for her husband's sprained ankle. "Why he thought he should be playing basketball like that at his age is a mystery," she tells me as I ring it up. "But I think he got what he deserved."

I just smile and nod, watching as Aunt Lindsey goes back behind her counter to work on prescriptions. "I guess it's good we don't all get what we deserve," I say absently.

Of course, I'm thinking specifically of myself. If I got what I deserved, I would probably be doing time in jail or juvi hall. This thought alone fills me with a deep sense of dread. What if that happened?

"Time for you to go to lunch," Aunt Lindsey calls out.

"Oh yeah." I nod nervously. "Can I pick you up anything?"

"I'll call in a sandwich at the deli, if you don't mind. I didn't have time for breakfast, so I'm starving."

"Do you want the first lunch?"

"No, I need to finish these orders first. You go ahead.

I've got a granola bar to munch on."

Still aware of the parcel in my pocket, I head for the bathroom. It's not unusual for me to take a bathroom break before lunch. I turn on the fan to muffle the noise, then pour the pills onto some toilet paper, which I wrap tightly around them, then tuck it into my pocket. Then I wash and dispose of the bottle as planned. Nice and neat.

I see my face in the mirror as I stand up straight, and it's flushed with excitement. Fortunately, my aunt didn't seem to notice. I remove the Santa hat, then go back out, hoping the woman with the prescription isn't back already. Thankfully, she's not. Now my only challenge is to pull off an innocent act when she returns for her pills. Can I do that?

I go outside and take in some long, cool, damp breaths. If I thought I was nervous about cheating on those finals, I'm sure this is way worse. And I still can't believe what I've done. It feels like my life of crime is off to a solid start, and I hate to imagine what else I might do now. I have a teeny-tiny thrill about pulling it off. But at the same time I'm really uneasy.

I go to the deli and order a bowl of turkey bisque soup, but all I can do is take a few bites. My stomach feels like it's full of hardened cement. I sit there by the window, watching shoppers hurrying along in the rain. Some are towing cranky-looking children behind. Some look merry, and others look harried.

Suddenly, a chilly jolt runs through me. What if someone has already figured me out? What if, unbeknownst to me, Uncle Russ really did install a surveillance camera and it's all been caught on tape? What if I end up going to jail? If I was worried about how my parents, friends, and teachers would react to the news of me cheating, how will they react when they find out I've stolen prescription drugs? How can I possibly explain my bizarre behavior? That I did it to maintain my grades? To get into Stanford?

I stand up quickly, realizing that I've made a horrible mistake. A huge and stupid mistake. Really, I'm too smart to do something like this. What was I thinking? It would be far better to just take the consequences for cheating than to be caught stealing drugs. Isn't it a federal offense?

I pick up my aunt's order and hurry back to the store. I know I'm early, but I don't care. I tell her that I thought if I cut my lunch shorter, she could take her break sooner.

"Oh?" She looks surprised. "Well, thank you. That was nice."

I want to ask her if the customer who ordered the OxyContin returned yet, but that would be a dead giveaway. "I'm going to run and wash my hands," I say instead. "They're sticky from lunch."

"You can use this sink," she calls to me, but I'm already halfway to the bathroom.

"That's okay, I'll just be a minute."

The next thing I know, I'm digging through the trash, trying to find that prescription bottle. Finally I locate it and unwrap it from its cocoon of toilet paper. I replace the pills, slip it into my pocket, and reemerge.

"I'm going to the backroom." She picks up the deli bag and peeks inside. "To put my feet up while I eat."

I put the Santa hat back on my head, trying to act natural. "Okay."

"Just yell if you need something." She pauses for a moment, looking curiously at me, and suddenly I wonder if she knows what I did.

I ease out a nervous smile. "Okay," I say again, wishing she'd just go eat her lunch.

"Are you all right, GraceAnn?"

Now I remember my flushed cheeks and wonder if I look guilty.

"You don't seem quite like yourself today. Is anything wrong?"

So, trying to cover my trail, I explain how I felt a little off last night and how my parents were pretty worried. "Dad even told me to take a sick day today."

"Oh?" She looks concerned. "Do you need to go home?"

I shake my head. "No, I feel better. I think I'm just kind of worn out after finals week."

"That's right. I forgot. How did it go?"

I shrug. "Okay, I guess."

She chuckles. "Well, of course you'd say that. Still keeping up those straight As, I'll bet."

"I don't know about that. But I'm trying."

"Well, it makes sense you'd be tired. And since you took a short lunch break, maybe you'd like to quit early today."

I nod. "Sure. That would be nice. Thanks."

As soon as she's gone, I replace the bottle on the shelf. Now if only the customer would come and I could ring it up and bag it and be done with it. Of course, I know this means I still have the Dirtbag to deal with. My only consolation is that school won't be in session for a couple of weeks. Maybe I can figure out a solution before then. Maybe Dirk will get hit by a train. Or maybe I will.

"**O**h, I nearly forgot," Aunt Lindsey says as she returns from her lunch break. "Miss Julia called this morning to order a few things, and I promised you'd deliver them to her. Do you mind?"

"Not at all."

"Maybe you could do it on your way home."

"Sure. How's she doing anyway?"

"She sounded better. But she says she's still pretty weak. Poor thing."

"Maybe I could give her a hand with the housework," I say absently.

"Oh, that would be lovely, GraceAnn."

We get busy for the next hour or so, and the woman who ordered the OxyContin returns, pays for her pills, and to my relief is merrily on her way. I'm so glad I didn't go through with my plan. But I'm still worried about how I'll straighten things out with Dirk. However, I keep reminding myself that I have a couple of weeks before he expects anything from me.

It's almost four, and the pharmacy has no customers. I've finished cleaning the bathroom, and all the shelves look nice and neat. "Why don't you head on over to Miss Julia's?" My aunt hands me a bag. "I'm sure she would appreciate your company, and it's pretty dead around here."

Relieved to get away from the pharmacy — and to put what I nearly did behind me — I gladly grab my coat and bag and tell my aunt good-bye. On my way out, I take a careful look at one of the video cameras near the front door. I think it's still the old fake one, but I'm not sure. I'd like to ask, but that might make her suspicious. Better to just keep going.

As I drive to Miss Julia's, I wish my life would return to the way it used to be. I wish I could turn back the clock and do it over — the right way.

"Come in, come in," Miss Julia says cheerfully as she opens the door. "Always a pleasure to see you, GraceAnn."

I hand her the bag. "You're looking much better." And she is. Today she is dressed more like she used to dress. A neat pair of black trousers and a festive Christmas sweater.

"Thank you." She smiles and pats her hair. "I made it to the beauty parlor this week, and I almost feel as good as new." She leads me to the kitchen. "I even made cookies."

"Good for you."

"Help yourself," she tells me as she sits at the kitchen table and lets out a deep breath. "I'm still a little weak though. I tire so easily."

"Would you like me to make you a cup of tea?"

"Oh, that would be nice."

So I put on the teakettle, and while it's heating, I visit with her and clean up some of the cookie-making ingredients.

"Thank you, dear," she says as I bring over our cups of tea. "You are such a good girl. Such a fine example of a young Christian woman. Your parents must be very proud of you."

I shrug, looking down at my tea uncomfortably. "I guess so."

Now we both sit there quietly, but I can feel her gaze on me.

"I did get accepted to Stanford," I say, hoping to fill up the empty space. "That made them really happy."

"Are you happy about it as well?"

I look into her faded blue eyes. "I guess so."

She purses her lips. "That doesn't sound very enthusiastic."

I try to seem cheerier. "Oh, I'm happy about it. I mean, it's really great." I tell her about my dad's surprise of taking me to visit the campus last weekend. "It's really pretty."

She frowns. "Is something troubling you, dear?"

I shrug and look away.

"I've been told I have a good sense about these things. I think perhaps it's a gift that the good Lord gave to me, but I can tell when a soul is troubled."

I bite my lip now, worried that I might actually start crying.

"Are you still pining away for that boy?"

I shake my head no.

"Would you like to talk?"

I consider this. I have a feeling I can trust her. And I really do want to talk to someone . . . someone who won't be devastated by what I need to say. Oh, I know she'll be disappointed in me. Who wouldn't?

"I am very good at keeping a confidence. I've heard lots of secrets over the years. I've never divulged any of them."

"Oh, Miss Julia," I blurt out. "I've done something really, really bad."

She reaches over and places her wrinkled, pale hand over mine. "Go ahead, dear, tell me all about it."

I begin by telling her about the pressure I've felt to get good grades. "And it used to come a lot more easily," I say sadly. "But I've been taking some really challenging classes . . . and then I went through that breakup with Clayton, and I kind of fell behind."

"In your classes?"

"Yeah. I started getting some really terrible grades, and even though I studied and tried to bring them up, it was like I was stuck. I knew that my grade point average was going to go down, and I got worried about college acceptance."

She just nods, waiting for me to continue.

"I'd heard that some kids were cheating. And then I actually saw a girl cheating." I tell her about the bracelet and how I took it from her.

"That was probably a good thing to do." She nods with approval.

"It seemed like it at first. But then . . ." I take in a deep breath, wondering if I can really admit this out loud. "But then I used it myself. I asked to retake the test, and I cheated." I swallow hard, looking at her. But her expression hasn't even changed. She simply nods.

"And then what happened, dear?"

So I tell her the entire story, right down to Dirk's threat of blackmail if I don't provide him with some OxyContin.

She blinks. "What a horrid-sounding young man."

"He is."

"So tell me, what are you going to do?"

Tears are trickling down my cheeks now. I decide to just disclose the whole ugly thing, and I tell her about how I stole the pills today.

"Oh dear!" Her eyes grow wide as she hands me a napkin for my tears.

I quickly fill her in on how I returned the pills. "And the customer picked them up and everything's okay."

"That's a relief. Oh my, GraceAnn. You do not want to do something like that. It could get you into all kinds of trouble."

"I already am in all kinds of trouble."

"Yes . . . yes, that's true. But you know two wrongs don't make a right."

I nod, blowing my nose on the napkin.

"So, dear girl, what are you going to do about this?"

"That's just the problem. I have no idea what to do. I don't know how to get out of it. I've gone round and round in my head, trying to think of a way out."

She looks evenly at me now. And I'm sure I know what she's thinking—that I should simply tell the truth and take the consequences.

"If I confess, I'll get into serious trouble. I'll probably get suspended, and I might not even be able to go to Stanford. My parents will be so disappointed. My friends will be shocked."

She just nods. "That's true."

"I don't know if I'm strong enough to go through all that."

"Killing your pride is a difficult thing, GraceAnn."

"Killing my pride?"

"That's what God expects us to do. Sometimes it happens over time. Sometimes it happens in one swift blow. But eventually, if we truly want to serve God and honor him, we have to let our pride die."

"Well, it feels like my pride is already dead. I'm so ashamed."

"That's good. It's the first step. Realizing in your heart that you are nothing—nothing without God, that is. With God you can become the best person you can possibly be. But only after you put that pride to death."

"And how do I do that?" Even as I say this, I know the answer. But I guess I don't want to actually say it out loud.

She smiles, tipping her head to one side. "I'm sure the good Lord will show you what to do, GraceAnn. I suspect he already has."

I notice the kitchen clock now. "Oh." I stand. "I didn't realize it was so late. I need to go. I have a date tonight."

"Well, thank you for visiting me." She slowly pushes herself up out of the chair, groaning as she stands. "Oh my, I'm afraid I sat too long."

I walk with her into the living room, waiting as she settles herself in her recliner. "You should probably rest."

She nods in a tired way. "If I don't see you before the holidays, I wish you and your family a Merry Christmas. I didn't even send out cards this year."

I lay her knitted blanket over her legs. "Thanks. But don't you think you'll go to the Christmas Eve service?"

"I hope so, but I told my friend Harriet I'll have to see how I feel."

"Well, I hope you get better fast. And Merry Christmas to you too." I slip my jacket on. "And thanks for listening to me today."

"Thank you for trusting me enough to share. I will be praying for you, GraceAnn. I'll be praying that you do the right thing. And I'll be praying that God will lead you."

I thank her again before I leave. As I drive home, I wonder if she was more shocked and disappointed than she showed. Does she think I'm a terrible person now? Or has she really seen so much that she can take my stupidity in stride? I do know this though — the next time I see her, she'll probably want to know what I did to fix this thing.

I remember what she said about my pride and how it needs to die. And if I want to be perfectly honest, I'd have to admit that I still care too much about what others think of me—and I know that's simply my pride. It will be painfully humiliating to confess that I cheated. In many ways, it will truly feel like dying. Like the old GraceAnn Lowery, the outstanding scholar, has been put to death. And then . . . what will I have left? How will I survive that kind of personal annihilation?

As I park my car, I wonder which is worse: suffering from this debilitating guilt or having everyone know what I did. Neither option feels good. I just wish there was a third option. Some magical way to shake this guilt and save face at the same time. And I should be smart enough to figure one out. However, I'm afraid I'm not.

## CHAPTER 14

When I get home, I'm surprised to see that someone has put up the Christmas tree. It's not a real one, but it looks like it is and even smells like it is when Mom douses it with her evergreen spray.

Several years ago, my parents decided this was a "greener" and safer way to celebrate Christmas. And although I like real trees better, I understand. Still, I'm a little disappointed to see that the faux tree has already been decorated. But I must admit it looks pretty and cheerful in an artificial way.

"I thought you'd wait for me before putting up the tree," I say to Mom when I find her in the kitchen.

"Last year you complained so much about the fake tree that I assumed you wouldn't be interested in helping." She closes the dishwasher. "Sorry about that."

"It's okay, and it does look nice." I get a vitamin water from the fridge, then notice Mom is dressed up more than usual. "Are you and Dad going out tonight?"

"Just dinner and then *shopping*." She gives me a mysterious smile. "*Christmas* shopping . . ."

"Oh." I open the water and take a swig.

"I haven't even seen you making a wish list yet, GraceAnn.

And we know you've been a good girl this year." She chuckles. "What do you want Santa to bring you?"

I shrug. "I don't know." This is an old game my parents still like to play, but I think I may have outgrown it this year. Also, I happen to know that Mom is wrong. I have *not* been a good girl. And the only thing I deserve to find in my Christmas stocking is a lump of coal. That's what my parents used to jokingly threaten me with back when I was little and being a brat. Oh, I never took them too seriously. But now it seems reasonable.

"Well, I guess Santa will just have to surprise you then." She winks.

"You guys have a good time."

"You too," she calls out. "You won't be out too late, will you? Not like last week anyway?"

"No. The movie probably gets out around ten. I doubt it'll be past eleven by the time I get home."

As I get ready for tonight's date, I'm thankful that I can escape my troubles for a while. At least that's what I'm hoping for. And what better way to do it than spending an evening with friends and going to see a new-release action flick. I know I don't deserve to have a really good time, but I'm dying for a break from all the turmoil bubbling inside of me. Even if it involves a knock on the head, I wouldn't complain about a temporary case of amnesia.

· · · · · · · · · ·

While Mary Beth and I wait inside the theater lobby and out of the rain and wind, which is really starting to bluster, the guys get our tickets. Mary Beth pops into the bathroom, and I'm just going over the snack bar's menu options, trying to decide whether to go for popcorn or an ice cream bar, when someone taps me on the shoulder. Thinking it's Bryant, I turn around and smile, but to my horrified shock, it is Dirk the Dirtbag . . . and he looks a little irritated.

"Thought you were on vacation with your family," he says with an ugly sneer.

"I—uh—I thought we'd be gone by now," I say quickly.

"So did you work at the pharmacy today?"

"Uh, yeah, actually I did. But I won't be working there next weekend . . . we'll be gone then."

"I don't care about next weekend." He leans forward, putting his pudgy face close to mine. "All I wanna know is did you get the OxyContin?"

I shake my head, swallowing hard. "I . . . I couldn't. I never even had a chance—"

"Look, I don't like being jerked around like this. We had a deal, and I expect you to keep your end of it."

"But that wasn't the original deal." Why do I bother? Why waste my breath? This guy is a moron.

"I gave you a break and you know it. I trusted you to keep your part of the bargain. You better not let me down again."

Now I see the guys coming toward us. Bryant looks slightly concerned and curious. "What's up?" He joins us.

"Just chatting with an old friend," Dirk says in a syrupy tone. "See you around, GraceAnn. Don't forget what I said." Then he ducks into the theater. Naturally, he's going to the same movie we picked. It just figures. So much for my temporary escape plan.

"What was that all about?" Bryant asks me.

I shrug.

"I'm getting popcorn," Jorge announces. "Anyone else?"

Distracted by the urgency to decide what snacks we want to

take into the movie, I start deliberating between the warmth of popcorn versus the sweetness of ice cream. Fortunately Bryant gets involved, and I temporarily feel like I dodged a bullet. As I get my popcorn and soda, I convince myself that there's nothing too weird about an acquaintance coming up to say hello like that. Really, Bryant has no reason to be suspicious. For all he knows, Dirk and I could be old pals.

Well, in another life and on another planet maybe.

As we find our seats, I spot the back of Dirk's big boxy head a few rows ahead of us. Just seeing him sitting there, imagining his smug face, makes me cringe inwardly. It's like he is going to spoil everything for me. Like he'll be this horrid dark shadow that will follow me wherever I go. Seriously, what were the chances I'd run into him like this? How was that even possible? It's like I'll never escape him. Like he's going to haunt me and hunt me down until I give him what he wants.

As the trailers begin, I almost wish I'd just kept those stupid pain pills. What a relief it would've been to have simply handed them over and ended this craziness. But not really. Deep inside, I know it wouldn't be worth it. Miss Julia might've sounded old-fashioned and slightly clichéd, but it's still true — two wrongs don't make a right. I just wish something did.

. . . . . . . . . .

I honestly don't remember anything about the movie. Well, besides the crook eventually getting caught. I suppose that's because I related to the crook more than I related to the hero and heroine. That figures. We go for ice cream afterward, and the others energetically discuss and critique the movie, something I usually enjoy participating in, but tonight I have nothing to contribute. Nothing at all.

"Are you okay?" Mary Beth asks me as we're in the ladies' room together.

"Huh?" I pause from washing my hands and look at her.

"You just seem kinda bummed about something. Is it Bryant? Do you wish you hadn't come tonight?"

I shrug and pull out a paper towel. "No, it's not Bryant. He's fine."

"I'm sure he thinks it's him. I noticed his face a few minutes ago. He was watching you, and you were just spacing out. Like you weren't even there. But I can tell he's feeling bad, and I'll bet he's worried that you're not as into him as he's into you."

"He's *into* me?" I toss the paper wad into the trash and then experience a flashback to earlier today, back to when I was digging through a similar trash can at the pharmacy, desperately foraging for that bottle. How disgusting.

"You know he is." She reapplies her lip gloss. "But he's trying to be cool about it. And you're acting like you couldn't care less."

"Well . . . I think I'm just tired." It's only part lie. The truth is, I *am* tired. I'm tired of lying. "Long day at work and all." Then as a smoke screen I tell her about visiting Miss Julia on my way home. But that just makes me feel even guiltier.

I attempt to act more cheerful on the way home. Bryant is driving tonight. Not his grandpa's cool Caddie, but his mom's Toyota. First he drops off Mary Beth, then Jorge, since he doesn't live too far from Mary Beth, which hits me as pretty convenient. Finally he's taking me home. But we drive there in silence. I'm so ready for this evening to be over.

"I think I'm getting the hint," Bryant says as he walks me to the door.

"What hint?" Now I replay what Mary Beth told me in the

bathroom. Maybe she was right.

"I'm guessing you only went out with me tonight because we pressured you into it. And believe me, I won't do that again." He shoves his hands in his pockets, standing at the bottom of the stairs that lead to our covered entryway. "Sorry to put you through that."

From the top step, I look down at him, and a huge wave of sadness washes over me. What is wrong with me? "No, I'm the one who should be sorry. I just wasn't myself tonight. That's all."

He frowns, then looks down, kicking a pebble off the pavers and into the flower beds.

"Really, I know I've been acting weird. And I'm truly sorry about that. I was miserable company. But thanks for taking me to the movie."

He looks up with a curious expression. "Did your bad mood have anything to do with Dirk Zimmerman?"

I let out a groan, then just shake my head. I so don't want to go there.

"You can be honest with me, GraceAnn."

It's starting to rain again, and I feel bad that he's standing out there where raindrops are pelting him. And yet it's not like I'm going to invite him inside. It's probably close to eleven, and I'm sure my parents have gone to bed. I point to the bench by the door. "Want to come up here for a bit?"

So now we're sitting on the bench, and I'm leaning over, staring at my feet and wishing I'd just sent him on his way. Really, what good can come of this? And I feel too tired to even think straight. How am I going to possibly talk my way out of this?

"I know Dirk well enough to know he's bad news, GraceAnn. I'm sure you know that too."

I just nod.

"So why was he being so friendly with you? That is, if he was being friendly. It was kinda hard to tell."

"You heard him," I say. "He was being friendly."

"Then why did you seem so upset about it?"

"Upset?"

"I saw your face, GraceAnn. You were obviously pretty distraught over something."

I press my lips together, wondering how I can get out of this. "Well . . . I was caught off guard. I mean, you can imagine my surprise . . . that he'd actually come up and talk to me."

"It was more than just surprise." He turns and stares at me. His brow looks deeply creased in the sallow porch light. "Something about your expression was all wrong. Almost like you were stressed or scared or something. I can't put my finger on it."

I roll my eyes. "Because there's nothing there."

"There *was* something. I mean, seriously, I can't imagine you'd be interested in a guy like that, but who knows?"

I laugh. But it sounds hollow and phony to me.

"But at the same time, I could tell you weren't exactly eager to talk to him."

"No . . ."

"So what was going on?"

I wish I could think of something, anything. Perhaps even something humorous, a way to derail this conversation. But my mind is blank . . . and spinning.

"I know Dirk is one of the guys who sells answers."

I try not to show alarm. "What?"

"You know, for kids who cheat."

"How do you know that?" I study him.

He shrugs uncomfortably.

"Have you bought answers from him?" I say this in a slightly accusing tone and immediately regret it.

"It's not anything I'm proud of . . . but yeah, I tried it once. Last year."

I stare at him in shock. "You did?"

"But I figured out real quick that it wasn't worth it. I mean, besides being outrageously expensive, I just felt like crud after I did it. It's not like I have the highest ethical standards, but I know right from wrong."

I flinch inwardly.

"Of course, I know you wouldn't be involved in something like that. But I suppose the thought ran through my mind."

I don't know what to say.

"I'm sorry," he tells me. "I shouldn't be pestering you like this about Dirk. You obviously just got caught in a weird conversation. And I suppose I felt a little jealous or something." He gives an uneasy smile. "And then you were acting, well, a little cool. I guess I put two and two together and came up with the wrong answer."

"Like I told Mary Beth, I think I'm just tired," I say slowly. "I worked today. And finals week . . . and all the studying . . . and thinking about Christmas. Maybe I'm just a little overwhelmed."

He stands. "That's totally understandable. And I shouldn't be keeping you out here like this." He sticks out his hand and helps me up. "Sorry."

"No." I look into his eyes. "I'm sorry, Bryant. You're a great guy, but . . ." I don't know what else to say.

"But . . ." He seems to force a smile. "That sounds like 'See you around, buddy.'" He lets go of my hand and steps back. "And I get it. Anyway, Lowery, it's been interesting. And I hope you have a good Christmas and — "

"Wait!" I grab hold of him. "Please don't leave like that."

"Like what?" He gives me a nonchalant look. Like I haven't hurt his feelings, when it's clear that I have.

I take in a deep breath, knowing I'm going to regret this. "Can I trust you, Bryant?"

He looks surprised but nods. "Sure. Of course."

I close my eyes and swallow hard. Do I really want to do this? He was almost walking out on me already. What difference does it make if I tell him now? Chances are he'll really want out if he finds out what I'm like. So why bother? Besides, hadn't I already decided I was done with guys and relationships and that I was going to put my schoolwork first? Why go down this path if I don't have to?

I open my eyes now, prepared to balk and make up some excuse. And yet I see something in his face like he really cares about me. And suddenly I want to talk.

"What is it?" he asks gently.

This is going to be completely degrading and embarrassing and painfully humiliating. But then I remember what Miss Julia said about my pride — and how it needs to die. Maybe this is the first step in putting it to death.

"Do you swear to keep my secret?" I ask nervously.

"You have my word."

I take another deep breath. "I bought answers from Dirk."

His eyes grow wider, but he slowly shakes his head with a look of disbelief. "Wow . . ."

And then I start to cry. Bryant hugs me, and we don't say much. But I feel just a tiny bit better. Like maybe there's a way out of this mess I've created. However, I don't go into any of the details. I tell him it's late, promising to fill him in more tomorrow . . . or Monday . . . or someday.

At first I'm relieved when Bryant doesn't call the next day. And it's not like I'm keeping my phone in my pocket. In fact, I'm keeping it turned off most of the time because Dirk has been sending obnoxious texts to me, and I'm getting worried he might start calling too. So I only check it a couple times a day.

But after three days go by without a peep from Bryant, I feel both worried and sad. I'm worried that he might not be as trust-worthy as I believed and that it was a mistake to confess to him. What if he tells someone? Worse than that, I'm sad because I really wanted to trust him. He seemed like someone who wouldn't let me down.

Consequently, I'm surprised when he shows up at my door on Tuesday afternoon. I'm even more surprised that he has a Christmas present for me. After I let him inside and we're sitting by the fake Christmas tree, he explains that his grandfather, the one with the cool Cadillac, had a heart attack early Sunday morning, and it's been touch and go ever since.

"I've been helping with my grandmother, taking her back and forth to the hospital, staying with her, and trying to keep her from stressing out since she has high blood pressure too." He sighs. "But they just did a triple-bypass surgery on Grandpa this morning."

"Is he all right?"

Bryant nods. "Looks like he's going to be okay. And I just took Grandma home, and she promised to take a nap. So I decided to run over here and see you." He points to the small box wrapped in red foil paper. "That's just something I found at the hospital gift shop, but it reminded me of you."

"I don't have anything for you. I just didn't think we'd—"

"It's okay." He eases out a sheepish smile. "It's kind of a joke gift anyway."

I frown. "A joke gift?"

He shrugs. "I guess you'll have to wait for Christmas to see."

"Oh . . ." I stare at the tree now, wondering what to say.

"So, I was thinking about what you said. About Dirk and everything." He looks around like he's worried someone might be around to hear us. But I assure him that both my parents are working.

"Anyway, I just wanted you to know that I understand," he says. "And I don't judge you. After all, like I told you, I've been there and done that myself. While I don't recommend it, I know how it could happen."

"Thanks."

"And as distraught as you seemed on Saturday night, I'm guessing that it's a one-time thing for you too."

I slowly nod.

"What I don't get is why Dirk was pestering you that way. Because that's what it seemed like to me."

I'm fully aware that I haven't disclosed all the details to Bryant, but at the same time, I'm not even sure that I want to tell him everything. Sitting here in the light of day and the light of the Christmas tree, I can almost make myself believe that it's all behind me. And then there's my pride . . . which I suppose is not really dead. Just wounded.

After a long silence, Bryant begins again. "I'm not trying to pressure you into talking, GraceAnn. But I am a pretty good listener. And I do know where you're coming from."

"I know," I murmur.

"And sometimes it helps to get things out in the open. I'm not a strong Christian like you—"

"Who says I'm a strong Christian?" I shoot back at him.

He blinks. "Well, I just assumed . . . I mean, since you and Mary Beth both go to church and—"

"I can't speak for Mary Beth, but I'm not so sure about myself anymore."

"Oh . . ." He looks disappointed.

"It's not like I've walked away from my faith," I say with uncertainty. "At least I hope not. But I wouldn't exactly call myself a strong Christian. I don't even think I know what that means anymore."

A crooked smile appears. "Me neither."

"Did you ever know?"

He gets a thoughtful look now. "I used to go to church with my parents. But I kind of outgrew that, and they quit going as well. But my grandparents are what I'd call strong Christians. And the past few days, with my grandpa in the hospital, everyone in my family has been praying for him. I even said a prayer for him this morning as he went into surgery." He shrugs. "It's the first time I've prayed in years."

"I haven't been able to pray for weeks," I confess.

We both just sit there quietly, and I wonder at this unexpected conversation. Who would've thought I'd be sitting here by the Christmas tree talking about praying with a guy like Bryant Morris? Of course, who would've thought I'd be doing a lot of the things I've done lately?

I point to his tattoo, which is peeking from beneath his sleeve. "Will you ever tell me about that?"

He shrugs again.

"Does it have some meaning? Or was it just a whim?"

"Well, since you told me your secret, I guess I can tell you about this." He pushes up his sleeve. "It's a phoenix; I'm sure you know what that is."

I study it more carefully, seeing now that it does look like a phoenix. "The mythological bird. Didn't it rise from the ashes?"

He nods. "Do you remember Jason Ritkins?"

I think hard. "The name is familiar."

"He was my best friend all through middle school."

"Oh yeah." Realization hits. "I remember now. He died in a car wreck a few years ago." I look at Bryant, and I can tell by his eyes that he's still very sad over this. "I didn't know he was your best friend. I'm sorry."

"Well, that's because Jason and I were kind of sideline guys. We were both determined to live on the edge. We'd started messing with drugs and alcohol back in seventh grade. You know, breaking all the rules."

"I guess I kind of knew that. That's why I thought you had the bad-boy image."

"Well, I did . . . back then." He traces his finger over the tattoo. "But when Jason died, things changed."

"You decided to clean up your act?"

He kind of laughs. "Not exactly. I was so angry about him dying that I went really crazy. I started doing everything I knew was wrong. Drugs and alcohol and whatever I could find."

"Why?"

"I guess I wanted to self-destruct. Like I blamed myself for his death."

"But why?"

"Jason and I were supposed to do something that night. At the last minute, I bailed on him, and he went with those other guys instead. And, well, you know the old story — drinking and driving don't mix." He shakes his head.

"But I still don't get it. How could that be your fault? And what if you had done something with him that night? Maybe you would've been killed in the car wreck too."

"That finally occurred to me. I had this revelation a couple years ago — it was almost like Jason spoke to me — and I realized that instead of ruining my life over something I had no control over, I needed to rise up for Jason's sake. I remembered how he and I used to make videos — crazy stuff, you know, skateboarding off of rooftops, idiotic stuff like that. But we had fun. And we'd talk about going to film school someday. And it was almost like Jason was reminding me of that. So I decided to clean up my act and try harder."

He points to his tattoo. "I got this as a reminder that I was going to rise up above that crud." He gives a sad-sounding laugh. "Trouble is, I don't always remember. I guess I'm still a work in process."

"Wow." I just look at him, surprised at how much more there is to him than I knew. "Thanks for telling me that."

"Yeah. It's not something I go around talking about."

I reach over and put my hand over the tattoo. "Well, you can talk about it to me, Bryant."

"Thanks. You know what they say . . . about how confession is good for the soul. Anyway, if you need to talk to someone about, well, you know . . . anyway, I'm around."

There's a long silence and I'm seriously tempted to spill my guts, but now he glances at his watch.

"Except that I told my grandma I'd only be gone thirty minutes, and it's already been longer." He stands and smiles down at me sadly. "I better go."

I feel a mixture of relief and disappointment. "It's good to know I can talk to you. And I will definitely keep it in mind."

"If it makes you feel any better," he says as I walk him to the stairs, "despite feeling guilty back when I cheated, nothing bad came of it. No one ever found out. Dirk never bugged me about it or anything. Mostly it was just a personal thing—feeling like I sold out for one stupid test. Especially since it happened after I got the tattoo, after I thought I'd turned it all around. I guess that's why I went into that slump and decided I didn't care about grades and school." He releases a wistful sigh. "Now I wish I hadn't gone down that road either."

"But at least you're going to make the best of the rest of the year." I smile optimistically.

He nods. "Yep. And that might help."

"Thanks for the Christmas present. Sorry I—"

"Like I said, it's kind of a joke." He grins. "And in case I don't see you again, Merry Christmas."

"Can I at least give you a Christmas hug?" I ask meekly.

"You bet!" He reaches out and wraps me in a big bear hug.

"Merry Christmas," I say as he lets me go. "And even though I haven't been praying much, I'll still say a prayer that your grandfather's health keeps improving."

"Thanks." He zips his coat.

"I see you're driving the Caddie." I nod out to the driveway.

"Fringe benefits," he calls as he jogs toward the car.

· · · · · · · · · ·

The next two days pass slowly and uneventfully. Mary Beth and her mom have gone to visit her grandmother in Washington. My parents are working as usual. And I keep my phone off most of the time and catch up on sleep and reading. But by Christmas Eve, I'm starting to feel a little bit more like my old self. At least that's what I'm trying to believe.

And for my parents' sake, I'm trying to act normal as we enjoy a quiet dinner Mom picked up on her way home from the hospital. I can tell they're tired, and I know that Christmas is never quite as festive for us as I imagine it is for other families. But for a change, I don't mind so much this year. I'm relieved there's no big gathering or pressure to perform.

After eating, we go to the candlelight service at our church, just like we do almost every year. Music is playing quietly as we find our seats, and I spot Miss Julia with her lady friend, smiling and waving at me. I can see a questioning look in her eyes, like she's wondering how things are going for me. I give her what I hope is a reassuring smile, then sit down.

I'm not sure if it's my imagination or not, but it seems like this year's sermon is aimed directly at me. It's about human pride and how earthly beings were hungry for God to visit them, but they expected him to come in the form of a powerful king, someone who could rule and reign and change the world from the top down. Instead, Christ was born in a manger, coming to earth as a vulnerable and humble infant. It reminds me of what Miss Julia said to me last Saturday. And I almost wonder if she didn't put a bug in the pastor's ear. Although I'm sure that's just ridiculous paranoia on my part.

I'm relieved when the service ends. And I'm thankful that

Dad seems eager to go. "We're going to open our gifts tonight," he tells me as he hurries us from the church and across the parking lot, where it's starting to rain again.

"We never open on Christmas Eve," I point out as we get into the car.

"I know," he says mysteriously.

Mom turns on the Christmas CD she put in the sound system and giggles in a mischievous way.

"What's going on?"

"You'll see," Mom tells me.

With "Jingle Bell Rock" playing loudly and the windshield wipers whipping furiously back and forth, I realize that my parents aren't going to shine any light on this right now.

Before long, we're seated around the tree. Rory is happily sleeping next to the fireplace, and we're all sipping the peppermint cocoa that Mom and I made. But then Dad stands up, holding an envelope in his hand. He's grinning like he's so happy that he's about to bust a gut.

"Okay, are you ready?" he asks.

I nod. "Sure. Ready for what?"

"For Christmas, we are going to spend the week at Big Bear." He holds up the envelope. "We have lift passes and a cabin, and it's going to be great!" He looks at me like he expects some wildly happy reaction. But I just sit there — just like the old proverbial bump on the log. And that's how I feel.

"Aren't you thrilled?" Mom says hopefully. "You love snowboarding, and we're talking about a whole week. And the cabin even has a hot tub." She sighs. "I know I'm looking forward to it!"

"Yes!" I try to pump enthusiasm into my voice. For their sakes, I know I need to show some excitement. "That sounds fantastic! I guess I'm just in shock. A whole week?" I smile so hard my cheeks hurt. "This is awesome!"

Dad looks relieved. "That's more like it."

"Dad did this for you," Mom tells me.

"For me?"

They both look so happy that I feel confused.

"We're so proud of your accomplishments," Dad says. "And I realized that this is your last year at home, GraceAnn. Your last Christmas in high school. And I got to thinking that we have to do something really over the top to celebrate. So Mom and I both went to work rearranging our schedules. And Dr. Stone offered me his cabin. And we three are going to have the time of our lives."

He's actually dancing around the living room now. "We're going boarding," he says in a goofy voice. "We're going boarding." Now he's handing Mom and me gifts, saying "ho-ho-ho" like he thinks he's Santa.

I can't help but laugh at his silliness. "But why are we opening presents tonight instead of in the morning?"

"Because we are so outta here in the morning." He hands me a big box. "Open this one first. You're going to love it!"

The first box turns out to be a really great-looking hooded parka. Creamy white with faux fur trim around the hood. "This is beautiful." I try it on.

"Your mom picked it out."

"The salesgirl said they're the hottest thing."

So we all open our gifts. I feel slightly apologetic that I didn't get my parents something grander, but they're appreciative.

"I'll have time to read these books when we're up at Big Bear," Dad says.

"And I'm taking these jammies with me." Mom holds the

flannel pajamas up with a big smile. "Cozy."

"Hey, here's another one for you, GraceAnn." He hands me the red foil-covered box. I'd nearly forgotten about it.

"Who's that from?" Mom asks.

"Bryant brought it by," I say as I hold it.

"Aren't you going to open it?" Dad asks.

"Yeah . . . sure." I start to carefully remove the paper. "Bryant said it was kind of a joke . . . whatever that means." Then I explain about his grandpa and how he picked my gift up at the hospital gift shop.

"That should be interesting," Mom says wryly. "There's usually not a whole lot to choose from in there."

I open the box to find a tissue paper bundle. Inside is a figurine. I hold it up to examine it more closely. It's a Christmas tree, with an elf clinging near the top of it with a funny expression as he puts the star into place. At the bottom of the statuette it says: *It isn't how high you go in life that counts, but how you got there.*

As soon as I read this, a huge lump forms in my throat. I know exactly what Bryant is suggesting by this. And if this is supposed to be a joke, it doesn't feel very funny.

"That's, uh, interesting," Dad says with a curious look.

"I think it's sweet," Mom adds.

Then, almost as if someone just blasted a hole into the side of the Hoover Dam, the tears just start flooding out of me. I'm sobbing and snorting, and my parents are looking at each other with totally bewildered expressions. And when I'm unable to stop crying, they begin to look slightly horrified.

"*What is it?*" Dad moves beside me on the couch, places a hand on my shoulder, and hands me a nice white handkerchief. He almost always has one in his pocket.

"Please, GraceAnn, tell us what's wrong." Mom sits on the other side and slips her arm around me. "What's going on?"

"I — I can't," I sob. "It's — it's too horrible."

Now they look even more frightened, and I cannot believe I'm doing this. That I'm sitting here, falling completely apart, and just totally ruining their evening. And it's Christmas Eve! What is wrong with me?

"No matter what it is," Dad says calmly, "it can't be as bad as it seems."

"It will help to talk about it," Mom tells me.

A part of me really wants to tell them . . . everything. But another part of me doesn't want to ruin their Christmas. It sounds like they went to so much trouble to put this trip together. And it feels wrong to spoil it all for them. I can't tell them. Not yet.

"It's nothing," I say quietly as I wipe my tears and blow my nose.

"Nothing?" Mom sounds skeptical. "You're crying your eyes out, and you say it's nothing?"

"Come on," Dad urges me, "tell us what's wrong. Does it have to do with Bryant? Has he done something to hurt you?"

I shake my head no, wiping my nose vigorously and trying to think of something — anything — to throw them off my trail.

"But it seemed like the statue triggered something," Mom persists. "Does it have to do with Bryant?"

I look down at my lap. "I guess so." Now I flash back to the last night we went out and how I was acting so weird that he almost gave up on me. And feeling guilty for lying (or manipulating the truth), I tell them about that incident as if it had never been resolved. "I just feel so bad for hurting him. But I know I need to choose academics over him. Having a boyfriend is such a distraction to my studies."

"Was he pushing you to neglect your schoolwork?" Dad asks. "That's not right."

I shrug. "Oh, I don't know. It was complicated."

Mom pushes the hair away from my face. "Well, it's pretty late. And I think you're tired. Things always seem worse when you're worn out." She looks into my eyes. "And maybe you're having a little PMS. Do you think? That can blow things way out of proportion."

"You could be right."

Dad looks hugely relieved. "Go on to bed, GraceAnn. I'm sure you'll feel lots better in the morning."

"And Dad wants to make an early start."

Dad pats Rory on the head. "This guy has a reservation at the Dog and Cat Hotel, but they don't open until seven. Although I want to be there as soon as the doors open. Then we can be on the road and make it up there with time enough to make a run or two before dark."

I force a smile. "Sounds good."

They both look much more at ease now, assured that their daughter isn't really losing her mind. And that life as they know it is not about to change drastically. That's when I decide that this might be my real Christmas gift to them. Making them believe that everything is just peachy keen — not spoiling their image of me or ruining their Christmas. I suppose that can all come later. For a while, I must be strong.

But when I'm in the privacy of my own room, the tears begin to fall again. I feel like everything is just crumbling, like I'm going down deeper and deeper, falling into this black hole and knowing I will never find my way out. Poor Rory doesn't understand why I'm so upset, but his warm tongue swipes at my tears. And as I bury my head in his soft, smelly coat, I remember when I was little and Rory would lick my tears, how he would make me feel better, and how the sun really would come out again.

How I long for those good old days. If only I could turn back the clock and do this all differently.

## CHAPTER 16

After we pick up breakfast takeout, I pretend to sleep as my dad drives us up to Big Bear. Mom plays her Christmas CDs and sometimes my parents discuss work-related stuff, but mostly the car is quiet and peaceful. I try not to imagine how different this morning could've felt—if I'd spilled the beans. I'm thankful I didn't. And on some levels, I think my parents would be thankful too. At least that's what I tell myself.

As we get out of Dad's SUV and carry our stuff into the cabin, I'm sure we look like a perfect little family. Like we're so successful and have it all together . . . have everything going for us. No one would guess that it's all about to go up in smoke. At least my part of it. And that will hurt my parents. But I'll play my role (academic senior who's going to Stanford next fall) until the end of this vacation. After that . . . well, who knows?

I play the happy camper for the next few days. Pretending to have fun even though I feel like there's an ugly black cloud hanging over my head. It takes me a couple of days to get into the hang of boarding again. But by the weekend, I'm in a fairly good grove. Unlike some academic types, I've always enjoyed athletics. I used to play all the sports, but eventually narrowed it down to volleyball and softball. Then last year I limited myself to just softball and an occasional game of golf with Dad. Maybe that was a mistake.

As I'm riding the lift up, I wonder if I was foolish to deprive myself from sports. At the time I was convinced that there was only so much time in the day and that studies were supposed to take precedence over all else. But now I'm not so sure. I think I was shortsighted. Because there's something exhilarating about making your body perform in sync with your brain. It's the ultimate high and I love it. Snowboarding is all about balance, and I realize now that I have been out of balance. Is it too late to fix it?

But I try not to think about it too much. Like when I'm riding down the mountain, so tuned in to the snow and the slopes and the basic elements like gravity and motion. It's like I can block out everything else in my life. And in those moments, I feel so alive and good and *clean*. But then the ride ends and the rush wears off, and I remember that I still have stuff to deal with. I feel dirty again. And sad.

It doesn't help that Dirk's texts and phone messages are becoming more frequent and more aggressive. Finally, as I'm taking a break on top of the mountain, waiting for the slope below me to clear some, my phone rings. I think it might be Mom trying to make plans for lunch, but I see that it's the Dirtbag instead. So I just decide to answer it. I'm hoping I can assure him that I'm really gone and that he should just back off.

"Well, it's about time you answered," he says in an irked tone. "Don't you ever return your calls?"

"I'm sorry. But there's nothing I can do for you right now. I'm up at Big Bear with my parents and—"

*"Big Bear?"* he says with way too much interest.

"That's right." I realize I shouldn't give him any more information, and fortunately this is a big, busy resort with lots of

different places to stay. Not that I think he'd come up here looking for me exactly. But after that weird confrontation at the
theater, I don't know what to expect from this jerk.

"So, your parents must be pretty well off then?"

"Oh, I don't know about that."

"Well, I do," he snaps. "Here I thought you were some poor
little poverty case so I cut you a deal, and it turns out that *both*
your parents are doctors." He chuckles in a creepy way. "You see,
*I* do my research."

"Hey, I never meant to trick you. You offered me a deal and
I took it. But if you want, I can pay you the original price
you—"

"No, no," he says quickly. "It's too late for that. I was really
glad to hear your parents are doctors, GraceAnn. I think you
and I could enjoy a nice business relationship. What with you
working at the pharmacy and having doctors in the family . . .
hey, it's a nice little setup. I just need you to cooperate a little
more. You know what they say, I scratch your back and you
scratch mine." He laughs like this is hilarious.

"Look, I'll be up here until Sunday. So it would be nice if
you'd quit calling and stuff. Because there's nothing I can do for
you up here. Do you understand?"

"Okay. No problemo. Like I said, we can work together,
GraceAnn. I help you and you help me. *Simpático* like."

"Right . . ." I roll my eyes and control the urge to pelt my
phone over the edge of the mountain.

"I can wait until you get back. In fact, I can wait until next
Saturday. And I'll be happy to stop by your house to pick up the
OxyContin." His voice gets chilly now. "But that's it. If you
don't deliver the goods on Saturday, I will pull the plug on you.
And when you get to school on Monday, you will be called to

the dean's office and everyone will know that you're a cheater and you can kiss Stanford good-bye."

I can't even respond to that, but that old sick feeling is gnawing at the pit of my stomach again. I know he's serious.

"*Adiós, amiga,*" he says lightly. "See you on Saturday."

"See you," I mumble as I snap my phone shut. Suddenly I feel the need to wash my hands. Or maybe even take a shower. Dirk is the slimiest guy I know, and yet I can't seem to shake him loose. It's like his talons just wrap more and more tightly around my life.

I slip my phone back into my parka pocket and zip it shut. Then I look around, making sure no one was close enough to overhear me. People are coming off the lift, one after the next, and the place is crawling with riders, but I'm pretty much alone over here.

I stand and just watch the slope for a while. The riders look small from my vantage point, gracefully gliding down, occasionally tumbling, getting up, and going again. Do any of them have the kinds of problems I have? Or am I just unique?

I know I should call Bryant. He's left a couple of concerned messages, and I can tell he misses me. I texted him about where I'm at, trying to make it sound light and cheerful, but I'm reluctant to actually speak to him. It's because I feel guilty that he only knows part of the truth. He thinks that, like him, I cheated just once. He thinks that the only thing troubling me is my sensitive and delicate conscience.

And while that's partly true, I sometimes wonder if I could put up with the guilt if I could somehow silence Dirk the Dirtbag. And the truth is, that bothers me a lot. It also bothers me that I'm so able to keep God out of the picture. It's like I've pulled this heavy curtain between myself and God, like I think

I'm getting away with something. And yet I know that's ridiculous. Delusional even.

On our last day here, I feel like I can't take it anymore — like I'm in some kind of pressure cooker that's about to blow. Everyone else around me seems to be cheerful and happy, and since it's New Year's Eve, they're in this constant celebratory mode. Naturally, that only makes me feel worse. Like I can't possibly keep up this charade. Keeping all this crud locked inside is beginning to feel like poison.

Even so, I tell myself to just wait. Don't spoil my parents' last day of vacation. They both seem so relaxed and happy. I just wish they wouldn't keep making references to me, mentioning how this is a celebration of my last year and my acceptance to Stanford.

"Maybe even Harvard," Dad adds as we're having dinner at the lodge restaurant. He holds up his glass to toast me. "Let's not limit our thinking."

Mom grins at him. "Wouldn't you just love to brag to Dennis about that?"

Dad gives her a sheepish smile. "Well, now that you mention it, I do get a little tired of hearing him going on about his boy. I wouldn't mind giving him something to think about. Maybe quiet him down a bit."

And that's it. I just can't take it anymore. Despite my half-eaten food, I stand. I'm sure I can't force down another bite. "Will you excuse me?"

They look surprised but naturally agree.

"I'm just not hungry." I set my napkin on my plate, just like I've been trained to do when I'm finished with a meal. "I think I'll go back to our cabin now."

"Are you feeling all right?" Mom asks with concern.

"I think it's cramps," I say quietly. Another lie, but I know it'll work.

She nods. "There's some Advil in the bathroom."

"Thanks." I force a weak smile. "And you guys feel free to stay as late as you want. Watch the fireworks and bring in the New Year or whatever you want. I'll probably just watch a movie, then go to bed."

They both seem to appreciate this suggestion. I'm sure they'd enjoy an evening alone. Feeling a tiny bit of relief, I head outside. It's dark now, but there are lights everywhere, reflecting off the snow. The festive mood is even more widespread now. People are milling about, and I can hear an occasional fire-cracker going off. And if things were different—if *I* were differ-ent—I'm sure I'd enjoy this as much as anyone else. As it is, I just want to escape.

Snow crunches under my feet as I make my way back to our cabin, and a lonely, hopeless feeling washes over me. Instead of going inside the cabin, I sit on the log bench outside and just look out over the snow. What am I going to do? Tears are filling my eyes again, hot and stinging, and I lean my head back, hoping to hold them in. I'm so tired of my weakness.

I look up into the dark sky, seeing stars that my tear-filled eyes magnify, making them look big and blurry and blue. Kind of like van Gogh's *Starry Night* painting. And I vaguely wonder if his inspiration for that piece was that his eyes, like mine, were filled with tears.

"Oh, God," I gasp quietly. "Help me." Hot tears begin to pour down my chilled cheeks, and I just sit there staring up at the sky, longing for an answer. Some way to put an end to this misery.

"Please, God, please help me." I take in a jagged breath and wait, hoping that God will reach down and do something.

But I know. Deep inside of me I know. God is there — and he wants to help me. But he is waiting for me to do something first. And so, just like that, I start to confess to him everything I've done. I begin by admitting to the actual offenses. My original cheating with Kelsey's bracelet. Then buying the answers from Dirk. Then I confess all the lies that followed. At least all the lies I can remember. And then I think I'm done.

But I know in my heart I've barely begun. A quiet voice nudges inside of me, urging me to confess why I felt the need to cheat and lie. "My grades seemed like the most important thing in the world. More important than you, God."

There it is. I've laid it out there for the King of the universe. And it is not pretty. I feel ashamed to think that something as shallow as good grades (something that's not even alive) meant more to me than God. Then I realize that good grades were about me . . . my image . . . my pride.

"I was more concerned with my image," I confess, "than I was with you." I take in a deep breath. "And that's because of my pride. My stupid, foolish pride." I sigh. I know it's like Miss Julia said. I need to kill my pride. Before it kills me. But I'm not quite sure how to do this.

So I cup my hands in my lap. And I imagine that I'm holding my pride in there — and my grades and what other people think of me and my acceptance into Stanford and any hopes of scholarships and all my scholastic achievements. I imagine placing them, one by one, into my hands. And it's a lot of stuff.

And then I hold this imaginary bowl up to God. "Please take these from me," I pray. "Do whatever you want with them. Burn them or smash them or bury them or whatever. Just please — *please* — take them from me."

I sit like that for a while, my hands lifted up to the sky. I'm sure I look like a dork to anyone passing by. But I don't care what others think. I simply put that feeling into my hands as well. "Take it all," I say to God. "I surrender it all to you."

Finally, I tell God that I'm sorry. Truly, truly sorry. "And even if my life gets worse, I will confess what I did to everyone and anyone. And not just select pieces of it either. I will tell the whole truth and nothing but the truth. And I will take the consequences that come with it. I don't even care who knows or what they think of me as a result. I just want it all out in the open. Beginning with my parents." I gulp to think of actually doing this. "But I'll need your help, God. Please help me to tell my parents."

I pray for a while longer, and it's weird but I begin to feel lighter and happier than ever. I don't just mean lighter and happier than I've felt since I started walking down this dark, twisted path. I mean lighter and happier than ever in my life.

I actually stand up and begin to do a happy dance. It's like this heavy load has been lifted, and I know God loves me and, despite what happens, I'm going to be okay. No, I'm going to be better than okay. I'm going to be great.

I feel so good that I consider hunting down my parents and just confessing the whole thing tonight. But then I realize that their reaction will probably not be as positive as mine. It's going to take them a while to wrap their minds around all this. And they have every right to be disappointed in me. I would be shocked if they weren't.

So I decide to wait to confess my transgressions to them. I'll let them enjoy one more night of bliss, ignorant bliss. I wish there was some gentle way to break it to them. And I pray again, asking God to lead me in how I do this. I ask God to show me when it's the best time to let them know their "perfect little princess" is a liar and a cheat.

I know it won't be easy. But I know it will be doable. And I know God will help me. And in the long run, it will all be worth it. Even if the only college I can get into is a community college. Even if the only job I can get is stocking shelves somewhere. Somehow God will see me through. I know it. And I would rather have a lackluster life that's guilt free than an illustrious one that's burdened with regret.

get up early the next morning. New Year's Day. I quietly dress, then slip outside to walk around. It's pretty quiet out here, and I'm sure most of the revelers from last night, including my parents, are sleeping in today. But that's okay. It's just nice to be up and out and feeling good and alive . . . and clean.

Oh, I know I still have a difficult day ahead of me. But to my relief, I'm actually looking forward to it. It's sort of like the way I used to feel before a big test. (Maybe not recently, but before I messed up my life.) Anyway, I have this sense of apprehension and anxiety, but I know it won't be long until it's all behind me. At least I hope that's how it will go down. The worst part of it — the telling part — can only last so long.

"There you are," Mom says as I come back inside. She still has on her pajamas, the ones with cats on them that I gave her for Christmas. She's curled up by the crackling fireplace with a mug of something hot in her hands. "Did you plan to hit the slopes one last time?"

I shrug and sit across from her. "I don't know."

"Dad's taking a shower. We decided not to ski today. But you can if you want. At least until noon. Then Dad wants to get on the road."

I just nod, picking at a loose thread on my jeans.

"There's coffee if you want. Boy, did I need some. We were up too late last night."

"So you guys really celebrated," I say as I go to the kitchen-ette to fill a mug.

"Did you see the fireworks?"

"I did," I tell her as I put the last spoonful of sugar in and stir. "They were really beautiful reflecting over the snow."

"So you must've been feeling better then?"

I nod as I sit down. "It wasn't cramps after all."

Dad emerges in jeans and a T-shirt, rubbing his hair with a towel. He comes over to join us. "You feeling okay, GraceAnn?" He peers at me with blurry-looking eyes.

"I actually feel pretty good."

"There's coffee," Mom tells him.

He gets his coffee and then we are all sitting in the small space by the fireplace, and I have a strong suspicion that this is my chance. But my heart is pounding and I can feel my hands starting to tremble. And then as Dad stands up to leave, I blurt out: "I have to talk to you guys!"

"Huh?" Dad turns and looks curiously at me. "What's up?"

"You might want to sit down," I say quietly.

Now he gets a somber look, nodding as he sits back down and waits for me to continue.

"I have something important to tell you, and it's going to be hard for you to hear this. And it's going to be hard for me to tell you. I actually wanted to tell you before we came here. But then I changed my mind because I didn't want to ruin this vacation. And I had a really nice time. Thank you." I pause, trying to swallow, but my throat is too dry. So I take a sip of coffee.

"What is it?" Mom's face looks paler than usual.

Dad's jaw is tense. "Please tell us."

"It started during finals week," I say. "No, actually, just before finals week. I'd heard that some students were cheating on exams. In fact, it sounded like a lot of them were. And I could tell that the grading curve was being affected because I got some bad grades, but the grades didn't really seem to match up with the scores—except for the curve. I figured it was because of kids cheating." I hold up my hands now. "Not that I'm using that as an excuse."

"An excuse for what?" Dad asks in a firm voice.

"For cheating."

Mom blinks and sets her coffee mug down with a loud clink. "You cheated?"

I nod. "I'm sorry, but I did."

"Why on earth would you—"

"Quiet," Mom tells him. "Let her finish."

So I explain about catching Kelsey. "And I planned to tell on her. I thought she deserved it. But she told me this sob story, that her stepdad was going to beat her or she'd kill herself if she got kicked out of cheerleading. And I believed her. So I didn't tell. But then I got this crazy idea. I still had her cheating answers, and I thought it was only fair to retake the test and use them."

Mom's brows arch. "So you did?"

I nod. "I felt horrible when I was done."

"Good," Dad says, like that finishes it. "You should feel horrible. You know better than that, GraceAnn. We've taught you that it's—"

"But it didn't stop there."

"You cheated *again*?" He tips his head to one side, like he really doesn't want to hear this, doesn't want to know what his "perfect little princess" is capable of.

"I'm sorry, but it gets worse." I take in a steadying breath, then confess that I bought test answers for trig and AP Biology.

"You paid money for answers just so you could cheat?" Dad asks.

"To get good grades."

"How much did it cost?" Mom's voice quavers with shock.

I quietly tell her. "But the guy said he was giving me a deal. Half price because it was my first time."

"I can't believe this!" Dad looks to the ceiling and shakes his head. "I just cannot believe it."

"I felt terrible the whole time." I explain how I blamed Clayton for it, how I'd been pining away over him and how my grades dropped. "It was like I'd fallen into this black hole and couldn't get out. I know it wasn't just Clayton. It was me. I wanted to keep up my image. So I kept going down into this black hole." I sigh. "And it got deeper and darker after I cheated."

"So you learned your lesson?" Mom asks tentatively.

I nod eagerly. "Absolutely. And I'll admit it took me a while to figure out what I was going to do about it. But last night it was all clear."

"How so?" Dad's brow is creased, and I can tell he's taking this a lot harder than he's showing. And a lot harder than Mom.

"First of all, by confessing to God. I straightened it all out with him. And for the first time since it happened, I feel like I'm going to be okay."

"Well, that's a relief." Mom picks up her coffee with an unsure expression. "I mean, that's something. I'm still shocked that you'd resort to something like that, GraceAnn. I've known something was off with you for a while. I suppose that's what it was the whole time."

"So you confessed it to God," Dad says in a stiff voice. "And now you've told us. What's next?"

"I have to tell the school what I did."

Dad's eyes open wide and Mom presses her lips together. I can tell they're not so sure about this plan. But they don't say anything.

"I know I'm going to get into big trouble. And I will probably get suspended. And my grades will drop. And I suspect I won't get to go to Stanford after all, or even USC."

Mom's face looks painful with disappointment. "Oh, GraceAnn!"

"It won't be easy, but I know it's what I have to do. And I'm prepared to do it."

"Now, wait a minute." Dad stands and starts pacing back and forth in front of the fireplace. Rubbing his hand over his chin, he looks very intense. He reminds me of a wild animal that's caged but wants to kill something. He turns and looks at me. *"Do you really want to do that?"*

*"Dan!"* Mom's eyes flash at him.

"I'm just asking the question."

"What are you insinuating?" Mom demands.

He gives her a seriously worried look. "I'm just saying that maybe she's taking it too far. After all, GraceAnn confessed to God. She confessed to us. Does she really have to confess to the school?"

Mom looks stymied. "I—uh—I, well, I don't know. But she needs to do the *right* thing."

"What *is* the right thing?" he asks her.

"Telling the truth," Mom says.

And now they are arguing about things like situational ethics and the bigger picture and the inequity of some students cheating and getting away with it while others suffer by getting low grades. And really, they are saying some of the exact same things that I had recently been telling myself.

I feel mesmerized as I watch and listen. I also feel guilty. My parents are fighting because of me. Then I remember something. "Wait!" I say as it starts getting heated. "There's something else I forgot to mention."

"What?" they both ask simultaneously.

I tell them about Dirk and how he is blackmailing me. "He actually expects me to steal OxyContin from the pharmacy and—"

"*What?*" Dad leaps to his feet again. He is enraged now. "He what?"

"Because he gave me a deal on the answers, he expects me to pay him back with OxyContin."

Dad shakes his fists in the air. "Who is this little sh—?"

"Oh, Dan!" Mom cuts him off. "It won't do any good to go flying off the handle like that."

"I'll kill him!" Dad seethes.

"Calm down," Mom insists. "You're just making this worse."

"I told him I can't do it." And then, wanting to be completely honest, I tell them about the day when I almost did it. "I knew it was wrong." I look away from their shocked faces. "But I was so desperate . . . I just wasn't thinking straight."

Dad sinks back into the chair, putting his head in his hands. "I cannot believe this. Just when you think you know someone. My own daughter. I work so hard . . . and this is the thanks I get. I can't believe it."

I look at Mom, and she just shakes her head sadly.

"I'm sorry," I murmur. Now fresh tears fill my eyes. I had really expected to do this without tears. But seeing my parents in pain like this—all because of me—cuts to the core. "I'm really, really sorry," I say in a husky voice. "I would do anything to turn back the clock. I wish I'd never done this. It's like Pastor Arnold says: Once you start going down the slippery slope, it's hard to get back up."

"I'll say," Dad mutters.

Mom comes over and puts her arms around me. "I can't say I'm not terribly disappointed. But we'll make it through this. Somehow we'll pull through."

"*How?*" Dad demands.

Mom gives him a blank look. "Well, certainly not by stealing pain pills and handing them over to the blackmailer. GraceAnn has no choice. She has to tell the truth."

"And lose everything? Just throw it all away? Everything we've worked for? Just toss it aside?"

"What other choice do we have?" Mom asks.

"I don't know." He runs a hand through his hair. "But it seems like there should be a solution. What if we offered the little thug money? Could we pay him off?"

"Oh, Dan!" Mom looks exasperated. "You'd stoop to his level?"

"To save GraceAnn's reputation? Her college career?" He shakes his fist again. "You bet I would."

"I know you're saying that because you love me," I gently tell him. "But really, I'm okay with this."

"You're okay watching your future being flushed down the toilet?"

"Sort of." I shrug. "Last night I decided that I'd rather put my pride to death and still have God than the other way around."

"Huh?" Dad looks confused.

So I tell him about what Miss Julia told me a couple weeks

ago. "I didn't really get it then. But I do now. I can see that my pride was all wrapped up in those stupid decisions. It was my pride—not wanting anyone to see me failing a class—that made me resort to cheating. It was my pride that got me into this mess. And to get out of it, I have to surrender my pride to God. If that means my future gets flushed down the toilet, as you say, I'll just have to live with it."

Dad just looks at me, slowly shaking his head like he thinks I'm hopeless. "I'm sorry, that might sound good and noble to you, but I think it's a bunch of poppycock."

"I don't," Mom tells him. "In fact, I can respect that."

"But what about her future?"

"My future is in God's hands," I tell him. "Where it should've been all along."

"And if your future is slinging burgers and living in a single-wide?" Dad challenges me.

"As long as God's with me, I'll be fine."

He just rolls his eyes.

"Go finish getting dressed," Mom tells him. "You're not making this any better."

He mutters something as he heads back to their room.

"I'm sorry, Dad," I call out. "I hope you'll forgive me someday."

But the only answer I get is the loud bang of the door closing.

"He'll get over it," Mom says as she goes to the kitchen and pours her untouched coffee down the sink. "Just give him some time."

I pour my cold coffee out too. "I wish it didn't have to be so painful for you guys. I mean, it's only fair that I should suffer. But it kills me to see how it hurts you."

She puts an arm around my shoulders. "Maybe our pride

needs to be put to death too, GraceAnn. Did you ever think about that?"

"But shouldn't that be between you and God? I mean, I shouldn't be the one who forces you to deal with your pride, should I?"

She shrugs. "God works in mysterious ways."

The ride home is even quieter than last week's ride to Big Bear. Only this time it's a lot more uncomfortable. It's like everyone's thoughts are floating around the interior of the car, like it's so thick that it's hard to breathe or think. Dad is really stewing. Like I did before I gave in to God. Dad is probably going through all the mental aerobics, playing out possible escape routes in his head, trying to find some magical way to cover this nasty mess up. But I know, in time, he'll figure out that there's only one way out. For now, I just let him stew.

I didn't know it was possible to feel good and bad simultaneously, but that is exactly what I'm experiencing today. On one hand, because I came clean with God and am able to pray again, I feel relatively freed up and relieved. On the other hand, this heavy black cloud is still hanging over my head, and it's overwhelming to think of how much is left to deal with.

We got home last night, and after picking up Rory, my dad, without saying a word to me, went straight to bed. And it was only eight. Mom said he was worn out from the trip, but I'm pretty sure he was worn out from me.

By the time I get up this morning, my parents have already gone to work. Since the sun is shining, I decide to take Rory for a walk. I can tell he's really missed me, and it's the least I can do to make up for his time at the kennel. Besides, walking might help me figure things out.

But this weird schizophrenic sensation continues as I let Rory off the leash in the dog park. I watch him take off running with abandon, enjoying this freedom, and I can totally relate to him. I feel incredibly euphoric . . . but a couple minutes pass and suddenly I'm overwhelmed with sadness and a sense of dread. This thing is so far from over.

For starters, I still have Dirk the Dirtbag to straighten out. I don't even know exactly how I'll do it, and I'm sure not looking forward to seeing him tomorrow. Although I do plan to go to work at the pharmacy. But I definitely have no plans to get him his stupid pills. But besides the Dirtbag, there's the school to deal with. I know I have to make a full confession . . . and take the consequences. That sure won't be easy. But nearly as unsettling as facing teachers and the dean will be confessing to my friends. Mary Beth and her mom won't be home until Sunday night, and I'd really like to have this conversation with Mary Beth in person.

As Rory and I are walking back home, Bryant calls and asks how I'm doing — in such a tender way that it makes me want to cry. And then I remember that although he knows a part of the story, he hasn't heard the whole thing yet. Perhaps he's a good one to begin with. Hopefully he'll understand. Or if he doesn't, at least I will have that out of the way. As pathetic as it sounds, I'm totally prepared to end up friendless after this whole thing plays out.

"I, uh, I'd like to talk to you. I mean, if you have the time."

"Sure," he says with enthusiasm. "Want me to come over?"

So we agree to meet back at my house in about an hour. Time enough for me to take a shower and get my head together. Oh, I know he's not going to freak out like Dad did, but I should expect the unexpected.

When Bryant shows up, I try to act calm and collected and I even thank him for his Christmas present, but inside I feel shaky. After we sit down in the sunroom, I initiate the conversation. "You remember what I told you about cheating," I say slowly. "Well, there was a little more to the story than what I told you." I go through the series of events and how I bought two sets of answers and how Dirk is now trying to blackmail me. "But I confessed the whole thing to my parents yesterday, and now I want to come clean with everyone."

Bryant doesn't look very surprised . . . or disappointed. But he doesn't say anything, and that makes me continue talking.

"So I just thought you should know the whole story. And even though it will be humiliating, I do plan to tell the school too."

"Because Dirk is blackmailing you?"

I shake my head. "No. Because it's the right thing to do." I decide to take this one step further, and I tell him about my breakthrough with God on New Year's Eve. "And even though it's really hard, I know God is going to help me through it."

He nods slowly, like he's absorbing this.

"Anyway, I'll understand if you think less of me. I know I think a lot less of myself now." I feel that familiar lump growing in my throat. But I really don't want to cry.

"No, I don't think less of you, GraceAnn. In fact, it's almost the opposite. You seem more human now. And I'm impressed that you're willing to risk everything by telling the truth. What about Stanford?"

I shrug. "I'm just taking this one step at a time. I have to trust God to work out the details. If I lose Stanford, I'll figure out something else."

"Wow . . ." He looks truly stunned. "That sure doesn't sound like the old GraceAnn."

So I tell him about Miss Julia and what she said about killing my pride a couple weeks ago. "I didn't really get it then, but I get it now." I let out a shaky smile. "And even though it's hard, I feel a lot better about myself." I force a laugh. "Although my dad's not speaking to me. And he's sure that I've thrown my life away." I sigh. "I think God might be dealing with him about his pride too."

"So what are you going to do about Dirk?"

I grimace. "I'm not sure. I'm not looking forward to it. I mean, I'll definitely tell him to forget about getting the OxyContin. But I know what he'll say to that—he'll take me down."

"How can he take you down if you're already taking yourself down?"

"Good point. But I really wish I could make my confession before he does whatever it is he's going to do to ruin me. Sort of like damage control, you know? But the soonest I can get in to talk to someone will be Monday morning. And I plan to do that first thing. But what if Dirk beats me to it? I mean, I can just imagine going in to see Mr. Peterson and he already knows. He'll probably think the only reason I'm confessing is because I know it's too late to do anything else." I hold up my hands. "But maybe that's just how it's meant to be, and I should get over it."

"Hey, isn't there some kind of anonymous informers' hotline?" he says. "I remember hearing about it a couple years ago—a way for students to report things like bullying or illegal drugs or cheating."

"That's right!"

"I'll bet it's listed on the school's website." Bryant already has his iPhone out and is searching for it. "Yeah, there's a phone number and an e-mail address." He points to it. "You could turn yourself in before Dirk has a chance."

"That's what I'm going to do." I stand now. "I'll write a confession letter and e-mail it."

"Maybe you should make a hard copy to take to school with you too," Bryant suggests. "Just in case."

"Good idea."

"Well, maybe I should let you get to it." He stands now too. "Hey, I almost forgot to ask how your grandpa's doing." I walk him to the door.

"He came home from the hospital a few days ago. He's doing good."

"I'm glad to hear that."

Bryant bends down to rub Rory's ears, then looks up and grins. "Anytime you need to talk, GraceAnn, I'm here for you."

I smile at him. "Thanks. I really appreciate it. I know this thing is far from over. It will help to have a friend."

He stands and nods. "You got it."

As soon as he's out the door, I race to my room, open my laptop, and begin constructing my confession letter. I write and rewrite and go over it again and again. I want to be completely honest and own up to my responsibility and my bad choice. But I also want to make it clear why I felt so pressured to cheat. I want the administration to understand that other kids cheating hurts the students who are trying to do things right. I am also careful not to mention any names. This is my confession. Not Kelsey's or even Dirk's.

When I think it's as good as it's going to get, I print out a copy and then paste it into the e-mail and hit Send. And just like that, it's done. My fate is sealed. Everyone at school will know what I've done in a few days. Again, it's that bittersweet feeling: painful, but good.

Mom gets home before Dad, and as I help her put away groceries, I tell her about what I did. She hugs me and tells me she's proud of how I'm handling this, but I can still see that hurt in her eyes.

"I'm really sorry, Mom. I know I've already said it a lot and

I'll probably have to say it a lot more, but I am really sorry."

"I know you are." She nods as she places a milk carton in the fridge.

"Do you think Dad will ever forgive me?"

"Of course. But it might take him a while to get over it. He had such high expectations for you, GraceAnn." She folds a shopping bag and sighs. "We both did."

"I know," I mutter.

"I'm sorry," she says quickly. "I wasn't trying to make you feel worse. This is hard enough on you . . . on all of us. I guess it'll just take time."

"When I was writing my letter today, I got an idea." I put a carton of cereal in the pantry.

"An idea?"

"I wondered what would happen if I wrote a letter to Stanford, to the dean of admissions, telling him about what I did and what I learned and how I'll never do it again and how sorry I am. Do you think they might consider forgiving me?"

She studies me with a curious expression. "I think it's worth a try."

"Okay." I nod eagerly. "I'm going to go do it right now."

"And at the very least, you'll have laid it all out for them. They should appreciate that."

My second letter is similar to the first one, but it feels good—almost therapeutic—to write it. Then I realize I owe my teachers an apology too. So I write confessional letters to both Mr. VanDorssen and Ms. Bannister, telling them exactly when and how I cheated and asking for their forgiveness. I put all these letters into white business envelopes, address them, and tuck them into my bag. Ready for Monday.

By the time my dad comes home, I'm feeling slightly

hopeful. But when we sit down to dinner, he is still frosty cold. Even when I tell him about what I'm doing, how I'm attempting to do damage control, he barely looks at me. And once again, he turns in early. I know he's not really going to bed because I can hear the television on in their master suite. I know he's just trying to escape being around me. Will he ever come to terms with this?

The next morning, I get up and dress for work, and before my parents are up, I go to the pharmacy. To my dismay, Uncle Russ is working today. I had really hoped it would be my aunt, because I suspect that she, like Mom, might be more understanding. And I know I have to confess what I've done to them as well. Even the part about the OxyContin, which I'm fairly sure will cost me this job.

It's midafternoon and there's a lull in business. With no customers in the store, Uncle Russ is making small talk with me as I wipe down the countertop around the pharmacy. This is my opportunity.

"I have something hard to tell you," I begin. He looks surprised and a bit wary but simply nods and listens as I pour out my embarrassing story. Even the part about Dirk pressuring me for pain meds.

Uncle Russ looks thoroughly stunned.

"I know you're disappointed. But because I'm confessing the whole thing at school and to everyone, it's only fair you should know too. And I'll understand if you need to let me go."

His brow creases. "Really, that's what you think I should do?"

"You know, because of that business about the OxyContin."

"But you didn't do it, GraceAnn. Or did I misunderstand that part?"

"No, of course I didn't do it."

He purses his lips like he's thinking hard.

"I'm really sorry, Uncle Russ. And ashamed. And I really do understand if you want to fire me."

"So, why would I fire you?"

I shrug, glancing to the door where a customer has just come in.

"The truth is, I did something similar to this myself once."

I blink. "Really?"

He nods. "I'm not proud of it. And I never got caught and I never told anyone. But I always regretted it."

"Seriously?"

"And it's always bothered me."

"I can understand that."

"So . . . maybe this is my way of making up for it."

I take in a deep breath, feeling the relief washing over me.

"You learned your lesson, GraceAnn. I can respect that." He pats me on the back. "Thanks for telling me."

"And you can tell Aunt Lindsey too. I want her to know."

He just nods. Now the customer is approaching with a prescription in hand, and it's time to get back to work. But my burden feels so much lighter for the rest of the afternoon. And when I'm done working, I decide to stop by to pay my respects to Miss Julia.

As usual, she is happy to see me. And she doesn't even seem terribly surprised when I tell her about New Year's Eve and how I've confessed everything to almost everybody.

She smiles. "Yes dear, I knew you would do the right thing."

"You did?"

"Certainly. I knew the good Lord wouldn't let you slip between his fingers. He has such good plans for you. This little bump along the way is just part of it."

"Little bump?"

She chuckles. "Well, I'm sure it seems like much more than that right now. And it certainly would've been much more than a little bump if you had let it go on."

"It was derailing my whole life. Even now I feel like I'm barely on course. I may have forfeited Stanford."

"Yes. That's understandable. But someday you'll probably look back and simply see this as a small bump along the way."

"I hope so." I hug her and thank her for believing in me, then head on home. Of course, it's not until I turn onto my street—and I see a sinister-looking black SUV—that I remember about Dirk.

It's Saturday. He's here for his drugs. I consider pulling over behind his car but then decide to simply continue into my own driveway. Let him follow me in there if he wants. At least I'm on my own turf. If he starts getting out of hand, I can make a mad dash into my house. Hopefully my parents are home, but it's hard to tell since they usually park in the garage.

I'm barely out of my car when his SUV comes zipping up behind me in the driveway and his tires screech as he stops fast. I head up the walk to the front door, pausing to watch as he leaps out of his SUV and hurries toward me. "You got it?" he calls out. "The rest of my payment?"

I shake my head. "No."

His face darkens and he comes closer. "Why not? I know you worked today. I drove by and saw your car parked there. What's the deal?"

I step back from him. "Because it's wrong. And because—"

"You are going down!" he snarls at me. "I've had it with you. I am pulling the plug, and you can kiss your fancy colleges good-bye."

"I've already done that," I say evenly, stepping away from him. "I've confessed everything."

He glares at me. "You think I'm going to believe that?" He makes a nasty laugh. "Like I haven't heard that one before? For a smart girl, you're pretty stupid."

"I was stupid to go to you." I step back again. "But I'm paying for that and—"

"And you better pay me too. You owe me and—"

"She does not owe you a thing!" Now my dad is out the front door. Wearing only sweatpants and with his hair dripping wet, he charges toward Dirk with his fist raised. "And you better get off my property before my wife calls the police and I start pressing charges."

Dirk looks surprised and scared as he backs up.

"And if you know what's good for you, you'll stop running this nasty little business. And you'll get out of town before it's too late." Dad narrows his eyes. "I have connections. I know people who can take care of low-life losers like you. And I'm ready to give them a call right now!"

Dirk gets into his SUV, backing up—fast. But Dad still stands there, shaking his fist in the air and looking pretty threatening. It's not until Dirk is gone that I realize I've been holding my breath.

"Thanks, Dad," I say quietly.

He presses his lips together and shakes his head. "What a jerk!"

"I know."

We both turn to walk back toward the house. "I appreciate you coming out like that."

He stops walking and turns to look at me. "What did you

expect me to do?"

I shrug, feeling that lump in my throat again.

"I'm your dad, GraceAnn."

I just nod, tears burning in my eyes.

"I might be mad at you, but I still love you." Then he takes me in his arms and hugs me . . . and the tears pour out . . . from both of us. Finally he lets me go and we head for the house.

"Do you really know people who could take care of Dirk?" I ask as we go inside.

He makes a funny grin. "No, but I could sure look some up."

I can't help but laugh over the image of my straitlaced dad making some new Mafia friends to go after Dirk the Dirtbag.

On Monday morning, I get to Mary Beth's house about twenty minutes earlier than usual. "Wow, you're really prompt today," she says as I wait for her to gather her stuff. "You must be chomping at the bit to get back to school." She laughs. "Unlike the rest of us."

"I came early because I need to tell you something." I glance around the kitchen. "Is your mom around?"

"She already went to work." Mary Beth frowns. "Is something wrong?"

And so once again, I tell my story. To my surprise it's easier than usual. Maybe because it's starting to feel sort of anticlimactic. I tell her the whole thing clear down to the incident with Dirk and my dad on Saturday and how my dad is finally talking to me again.

However, when I'm done, I'm taken aback at Mary Beth's expression. It seems like a mixture of surprise and something else . . . like disgust.

"I cannot believe you'd do that," she says in a wounded tone.

"I couldn't believe it either."

"I mean, that you kept it from me. I knew something was up with you, and I asked you over and over to talk about it. But you refused." She frowns. "I thought I was your best friend."

"You are. But I didn't want to tell *anyone*."

"But this is me, GraceAnn. We tell each other everything."

"I know . . . but this was so terrible . . . and so humiliating. I just couldn't talk about it. Not even to God. I kept hoping that it would all just go away. But instead it snowballed, getting worse and worse. I kept trying to think of some way out—a way to keep it hidden. I didn't want *anyone* to know."

"Even so." She folds her arms across her front. "It's like I'm the last one to hear about it."

"I'm sorry. But you were gone when I finally decided to come clean. And then I wanted to tell you face-to-face."

As we get into my car, I can't think of anything else to say. I can't believe she's taking this so personally. And then it hits me—it's her pride. "You know," I begin carefully as I start to drive, "I used to have a lot of pride. Especially when it came to academics. But I learned that my pride was a bad thing." Now I tell her about what Miss Julia said. "I'm having to put my pride to death."

"Oh . . ."

"Anyway, I'm sorry you feel hurt by this, Mary Beth. And I wish my pride hadn't gotten in the way of me telling you. I really needed someone to talk to. And from now on I'll make sure to come to you first. I mean . . . after God."

She nods. "Well, I'm glad you told me now. Sorry to go on like that, but it's like you've been living this secret life, and I'm supposed to be your best friend. And I never keep secrets from you."

"Point taken. Now, since you're my best friend, can I ask you to pray for me when I go into Mr. Peterson's office?"

"Sure."

I take in a slow, deep breath. "This is not going to be easy."

· · · · · · · · · ·

Mr. Peterson is sitting at his big shiny desk with my opened letter in front of him and a very disturbed frown across his face. "I can't pretend I'm not shocked by this, GraceAnn." He refolds the letter and slips it back into the envelope. "You're the last student I expected this from."

I nod. "I know."

He shakes his head. "School policy is that anyone caught cheating will face immediate suspension. For two weeks."

"I know."

"Naturally, your teachers will have to be informed."

"I know."

He removes his glasses, rubbing the bridge of his nose as he peers curiously at me. "Do you mind revealing who your source is?"

I shrug. "Not really. I mean I wish he'd get caught. He ruins it for everyone. And he's really a thug. But I guess I'm a little worried that he might try to take out his revenge on me. He's kind of a scary dude." Although as I recall the frightened look in his eyes when my dad came after him, I think maybe he'll leave me alone.

"Is it a fellow student?"

I shake my head. "An ex-student."

"Uh-huh." Mr. Peterson looks evenly at me. "It might go better for you, and everyone, if you tell me."

So I tell him. And I give him Dirk's phone number and vehicle description and even the e-mail address he used to send me the answers. Mr. Peterson writes all this down, then seems eager to get rid of me.

"Should I go home now?" I ask as I gather my bag and coat.

He looks perplexed. "No. Not just yet. Go on to class. It looks like you can make it on time to second period, and I'll get back to you in regard to your, uh, punishment. If you don't hear from me before noon, come on back here and we'll talk again."

"Okay. I really am sorry," I say as I reach for the door. "Sorrier than I can even say."

He nods. "I know you are."

I feel a tiny bit hopeful as I go to class. Oh, I know that I'll probably still get suspended. Like Mr. Peterson said, rules are rules and they can't bend them—even if I am normally an exceptional student. I get that. But I guess I'm relieved that Mr. Peterson didn't seem to hate me. And it feels good knowing that they might go after Dirk. I hope they can catch him. Even if it means I have to go into hiding. That shouldn't be too difficult since I won't be at school anyway. In fact, it might be a relief. Or is that just my pride talking again?

Before I go to my second class, I stop by trig and hand Mr. VanDorssen my letter. "What's this?" He grins. "A fan letter?"

I force a smile. "I wish." Then I turn and hurry away.

I also stop by to give Ms. Bannister her letter. She's just coming out of the classroom and looks a bit surprised, but she takes it and slips it into her book bag. "See you later."

"I hope so," I tell her, then hurry on my way.

Finally, after what feels like the longest morning ever, I am walking back toward administration, ready to be sentenced. It feels like I'm taking in this school for the last time. Maybe that's how a convict feels as he's being taken to his execution. Like I'm trying to see everyone and everything, pasting the snapshots in my mind.

"Just who I was looking for," Mr. Peterson says as I come into the administration center. He waves me over to his office.

"Right this way, Miss Lowery."

With what feels like a brick in the pit of my stomach, I sit down again, ready to hear my sentencing.

"Well, I've discussed your situation with the principal and the counselor and even gotten some feedback from several of your teachers, GraceAnn. And we have reached a consensus."

"A consensus."

He nods. "We all agreed the rule states that any student *caught* cheating will face suspension. And we all agreed that you never got caught. You turned yourself in."

I blink, feeling slightly light-headed. "So I won't be suspended?"

"No. But we did agree on some disciplinary measures. First of all, you will be required to provide twenty hours of tutoring service. But you have until graduation to finish it up. Do you think you can manage that?"

"Sure, I'd be happy to."

"And, of course, you'll receive Fs for the three tests you cheated on. I'm sure that goes without saying. Your GPA will drop as a result."

"Of course." I nod eagerly.

"We think your cooperation will help us to implement a major crackdown on all the cheating that's been going on around here. It's been an item of growing concern this year. And having Dirk Zimmerman shut down should help things immensely."

"I sure hope so."

"So despite the circumstances, we do owe you some thanks, GraceAnn."

I feel embarrassed by this. "You mean because I cheated?"

"I mean because you came forward."

"Right."

"But that's not all. There's one more disciplinary measure, and I strongly urge you to consider it." He clears his throat. "I know it will ruin your image—and we can't force you to cooperate—but we plan to have an assembly later this week. We want to address this whole cheating business up front and openly. And we'd like you to speak to the student body. If you could reiterate what you wrote in your letter, tell your fellow students what you've learned and how you know personally that cheating hurts everyone and how you will never do it again, we'd be most appreciative. Would you be willing to do that?"

I think hard about how it will feel to stand in front of the entire school and confess what a fool I've been—how I disliked cheaters so much and how I became one myself. Talk about a blow to my pride. Still, I know it's something I must do. "Yes. I want to do that."

He smiles. "Great."

"In your letter you mentioned that you've ruined your chances of going to Stanford now—and that you'd written them a letter. Is that correct?"

I pull the letter that's already stamped and addressed from my bag, holding it up. "I planned to send it today."

"Are you sure you want to do that, GraceAnn?"

"I think I should."

"Do you realize that not everything on your school record gets passed on with college applications?"

I just shrug. "I guess I never really thought about it."

He stands and reaches for the letter. "Anyway, why don't you let me send it for you?"

"Okay." I hand him the letter.

Then, to my surprise, he inserts my letter into the shredder attached to the trash can next to his desk. There's a growling noise and the letter is gone. He turns to me and grins. "That takes care of that."

I can hardly believe it. But I simply nod, thanking him as I stand.

"Suffice it to say, we think you've learned your lesson, GraceAnn." He opens the door for me. "The hard way."

"That's for sure."

He reaches out and shakes my hand. "And now you will share your hard-learned lesson with others, and perhaps we'll get a handle on this dilemma."

"I'll do whatever I can."

I feel slightly dazed as I head for the cafeteria. For the first time in weeks, I actually feel hungry. And almost completely happy, although there's still the assembly thing to grapple with and the humiliation that will come with that. But I can't wait to tell my friends—and my parents, too. How is it possible that everything changed so dramatically? That something so horrible could turn out okay . . . maybe even good? Who knew?

That's when I realize that *God knew* and that it's because of God that I survived this ordeal—an ordeal of my own making. Not only have I survived, but because of God, good things might actually come out of it. And I realize that there's no hole so dark or so deep that God can't reach down and pull someone out of it. And right then and there, I pause to give God thanks for rescuing me. I thank him for saving me from my stupid pride—and giving me a second chance!

1. First impressions are important because they are lasting, but sometimes they are wrong. What was your first impression of GraceAnn? Was it right or wrong? Explain.
2. Did GraceAnn seem like the kind of person who would resort to academic cheating? Why or why not?
3. Why do you think academic cheating is so prevalent in schools these days?
4. What was your first impression of Bryant? Was it right or wrong? Explain.
5. GraceAnn put a lot of pressure on herself to be perfect. Why do you think that was so important to her? Can you relate to that? Why or why not?
6. What do you think GraceAnn's parents might have done differently to help her in this situation?
7. Were you surprised when GraceAnn stole the OxyContin from the pharmacy? Describe what you think would have happened if she'd given it to Dirk.
8. Miss Julia plays an unexpected but much-needed role as friend to GraceAnn. Do you have someone like that in your life? If not, how could you go about finding that kind of friend?

9. GraceAnn eventually realizes that her pride is a problem. Describe the role that pride plays in your life. Is it helpful or hurtful? Why?

10. If GraceAnn's school really had a zero-tolerance policy for cheating, do you think it was fair that she escaped suspension? Why or why not?

11. How did you feel when GraceAnn's dean shredded her letter to Stanford? Do you think that was the right thing to do?

12. Did this story change any of your opinions about cheating or people who cheat? Explain.

## A SPECIAL ACKNOWLEDGMENT

**S**pecial thanks to Susan Brooks for submitting her character description of GraceAnn to the Melody Carlson Create a Character Contest. Participants of the competition were asked to provide a description of the main character, including her name, family life, friends, job, hobbies, and more. I loved reading the submissions and was impressed with how creative they were. It was really hard to choose a winner, but Susan's stood out to me.

One of the elements of Susan's character description that caught my attention was the main character's job working Saturdays in the pharmacy. This lent some interesting developments in the plot that I hadn't considered before. I also liked that GraceAnn had a friend like Miss Julia. I enjoy writing about older people and thought it would be an interesting relationship to develop.

So many ingredients go into a book — it's fun when someone else tosses a few unexpected ones in.

MELODY CARLSON has written more than two hundred books for all age groups, but she particularly enjoys writing for teens. Perhaps this is because her own teen years remain so vivid in her memory. After claiming to be an atheist at the ripe old age of twelve, she later surrendered her heart to Jesus and has been following him ever since. Her hope and prayer for all her readers is that each one would be touched by God in a special way through her stories. For more information, please visit Melody's website at www.melodycarlson.com.

# Lonely? Jealous? Hurt?
# Melody Carlson addresses the
# issues you face today.

## The TRUECOLORS Series

The TRUECOLORS series addresses issues that most affect teen girls. By taking on these difficult topics without being phony or preachy, best-selling author Melody Carlson challenges you to stay true to who you are and what you believe.

9781576835296

**Dark Blue**
(Loneliness)
9781576835296

**Faded Denim**
(Eating Disorders)
9781576835371

**Deep Green**
(Jealousy)
9781576835302

**Bright Purple**
(Homosexuality)
9781576839508

**Torch Red**
(Sex)
9781576835319

**Moon White**
(Witchcraft)
9781576839515

**Pitch Black**
(Suicide)
9781576835326

**Harsh Pink**
(Popularity)
9781576839522

**Burnt Orange**
(Drinking)
9781576835333

**Fool's Gold**
(Materialism)
9781576835340

**Blade Silver**
(Cutting)
9781576835357

**Bitter Rose**
(Divorce)
9781576835364

9781576835319

9781576835302

9781576835364

To order copies, call NavPress at
**1-800-366-7788** or log on to
**www.NavPress.com.**

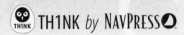

# MY LIFE IS **TOUGHER** THAN MOST **PEOPLE REALIZE.**

I TRY TO KEEP EVERYTHING IN BALANCE: FRIENDS, FAMILY, WORK, SCHOOL, AND GOD.

IT'S NOT EASY.

I KNOW WHAT MY PARENTS BELIEVE AND WHAT MY PASTOR SAYS.

BUT IT'S NOT ABOUT THEM. IT'S ABOUT ME...

ISN'T IT TIME I OWN MY FAITH?

THROUGH THICK AND THIN, KEEP YOUR HEARTS AT ATTENTION, IN ADORATION BEFORE CHRIST, YOUR MASTER. BE READY TO SPEAK UP AND TELL ANYONE WHO ASKS WHY YOU'RE LIVING THE WAY YOU ARE, AND ALWAYS WITH THE UTMOST COURTESY. 1 PETER 3:15 (MSG)

www.navpress.com | 1-800-366-7788   TH1NK *by* NAVPRESS

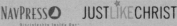

# The Message Means Understanding

*Bringing the Bible to all ages*

*The Message* is written in contemporary language that is much like talking with a good friend. When paired with your favorite Bible study, *The Message* will deliver a reading experience that is reliable, energetic, and amazingly fresh.

To find *The Message* that is right for you, go to **www.navpress.com** or call **1-800-366-7788**.

NAVPRESS

Discipleship Inside Out™

HELPING STUDENTS
**KNOW CHRIST
THROUGH
HIS WORD**

## What will YOUR STUDENTS do this summer?

## Choose from **TWO** great options.

### STUDENT LIFE CAMP

- Engaging worship from experienced worship leaders

- Learning through sound biblical teaching and Bible study

- Community in family groups

- Freedom for you to focus on your students

### STUDENT LIFE MISSION CAMP

- Repairing homes, landscaping, painting, and other work projects

- Serving food, organizing donations, and helping at homeless shelters

- Visiting nursing homes and mental health centers

- Leading children's activities and teaching Bible stories to children

For more information on Student Life Camps and Mission Camps, go to **studentlife.com** or call **1-800-718-2267**.